EVIL
NEVER
DIES

EVIL
NEVER
DIES

Mick Ridgewell

A
Grinning Skull Press
Publication
PO Box 67, Bridgewater, MA 02324

DEDICATION

For Wally and Norma Ridgewell, my mom and dad. Thank you for giving me life and providing me with all the tools I needed to make my stories possible.
And for Gerry and Betty Langlois, for being there whenever we needed you. You have been my second mom and dad since the day I said "I do," and for that, I am blessed

Contents

ACKNOWLEDGMENTS

Special thanks to Pam Bone, Roy James, Mike Soucie, and Greg Toldo. This is a better book thanks to your excellent advice and suggestions.

A big shout out to my critiquing group, Write On Windsor, for all the tips and support, past and present.

I am indebted to Don D'Auria for believing in me and giving my work a chance.

And lastly, I greatly appreciate the entire staff of Grinning Skull Press for giving this book of death a new life.

Chapter 1

Roland Millhouse had his eyes on the prize. He would be a field reporter for a couple more years, and then make his play for the anchor desk in Toronto. Maybe, if all the planets lined up, he would follow Peter Jennings's path all the way to New York.

When Roland was assigned to drive six hours north to interview Patricia Owens, Canada's oldest living citizen, he went without protest. He really did hold himself to standards far above mere fluff bits, but Roland took whatever assignment came his way. You don't get in favour with the movers and shakers by being a prima donna.

The thought of trying to get a coherent response from a 120-year-old woman made his lunch sour in his stomach. Roland had grudgingly spent enough time visiting his grandmother in the nursing home. He adored his grandmother growing up, but by the time she checked into that place, there was little left of her mind. Memories of those visits gave him preconceived notions of what this assignment would be like. He pictured oxygen tubes in her nose and the smell of her filth as she sat in soiled diapers.

Getting his first glimpse of the Owens house didn't improve Roland's impression of this assignment. Putting his car in park in front of the place, he had to crane his neck over the steering wheel to see the whole structure, and as he did so, *The Addams Family* theme song began to play inside his head.

Creepy and kooky indeed, he thought.

The house, no doubt the toast of the county in its day, now looked haunted. The siding was bluish-grey. Unless you'd seen it many years ago, it would be impossible to say if it had been blue or grey. Now, ugly was the only word to describe this color.

Two and a half stories of ugly. Tall narrow windows filled the front of the house and were surrounded by white trim and shutters that were long faded to the shade of old bones. The ornate trim that adorned the eaves surely gave the house stately elegance decades ago, but now only reminded the viewer of the damage time and the elements will inflict on everything.

"Christ," Roland uttered, looking up at what one could only describe as decay.

Sickly roses tried in vain to thrive in a garden alive with all manner of weeds. The lawn, although cut to a respectable length, looked to be all crabgrass and dandelions.

Roland's gut told him to get the hell out. They could send any flunky to snap a few shots of the old bag, sing her Happy Birthday, and wish her many more. It wasn't like she hadn't already had more than her share as far as he was concerned.

Roland always followed his gut when it pushed him toward a story, but he never followed anything, be it intuition or bad vibes that steered him away from one, not even a lame-ass birthday yarn for an old woman. He would take some snapshots, sing Happy Birthday if she could stay awake, then book it back to Toronto.

He checked his perfectly coifed blond news anchor hair, in the rear-view. Tightened his paisley silk tie then pulled the handle to open the door to his steel-blue BMW. Roland loved his Bimmer. When the sun was out, he could stand back and see his own reflection in the paint, and that is exactly what he did.

His image got a bit distorted where the contours of the car changed, but he brushed his Armani suit flat where it had bunched up in the car and admired first himself, then the shine on the car.

It was time to go to work. Roland retrieved his laptop and camera bag from the backseat and trundled across the gravel to the house. He paused at the first step leading to the porch, made an audio memo in his BlackBerry to photograph the house before he left, then climbed the wooden steps to the front door.

Something he thought could have been a pinecone carved from mahogany dangled on a rusted chain to the left of the door. He had seen these things in movies and television, but this was the first time Roland had to pull on a weight dangling from a chain to ring the doorbell. The chain made a dry grinding noise, followed by what could have been a couple of saucepans rattling together. When he released the chain, the weight clunked back to its original position with a thud.

He waited, admiring the Italian leather of his shoes. Most people would be taking everything in, having never been to a house like this, but not Roland. He was only interested if there was a story to be had, and he didn't see one here. Roland saw only a waste of his time and talents.

After what he decided was ample time to answer the door, but no more than thirty seconds, he reached for the pinecone. Before he could pull the chain again, he heard the door handle click, and the big wooden door opened with a screech that would have made the sound-effects guys of any horror movie set proud.

"Are you Mr. Millhouse?" came a raspy, but not at all unsteady voice.

Roland looked to find a tiny woman, no more than five feet, probably four ten, dressed in slacks and a white blouse, with small white flowers embroidered above her breasts. She was pale, but not in the way sick people look pale. Her skin was china white and as clear as new snow. She had her share of wrinkles, but not a hint of spots or blemishes that many very old people have. In fact, Roland was sure in younger days this old woman was attractive.

"Yes, is Mrs. Patricia Owens at home?" *Of course she's home,* he thought. The woman is 120, where is she going to go?

"I am," the woman before him said.

Roland thought himself a good judge of his surroundings when he wanted to be. The temperament of the people around him, their income bracket, and definitely their age. The woman before him could not have been more than seventy, maybe a very well-kept eighty.

"No, ma'am, I'm looking for Mrs. Patricia Owens. It's her birthday. Her 120th birthday."

"I am Patricia Owens, and my birthday is actually tomorrow. I'll be one hundred and twenty years old. Imagine that, if you can."

"I truly can't, Mrs. Owens."

"First things first, Mr. Millhouse," Patricia said. "It's Miss Owens. I never did marry. And, if you are going to get invited into my house, you will have to call me Patricia. I'm too damn old to be Miss Anybody. Wouldn't you say?"

"You're the boss, Patricia. And fair is fair, you should call me Roland," he replied. With that, Roland knew two things. He liked Patricia, and this wasn't going to be the dud assignment he had been dreading. What he didn't know was it would be the best story he would ever get.

"Patricia, can I take a picture of you on the porch before we go inside?" With a nod and a sheepish wave of her hand, Patricia stood in the doorway, waiting for her guest to get his gear ready.

He removed his camera from the case and snapped half a dozen pictures. He asked her to turn this way and that, explaining lighting and background. Once convinced he had a usable photo he packed the camera away, hung the camera bag strap over his shoulder and leaped back up beside her.

"Good, then. Shall we go inside?" Patricia said and motioned to the door.

Roland held it open until his host passed, then followed her inside.

Chapter 2

Roland looked around in awe, as if crossing Patricia's threshold transported him back in time. Deep patterned rugs all but concealed the hardwood floors, gaudy paper covered the walls, and the pale light from ornate wall sconces cast weak shadows all around.

On the walls, oil paintings from years long gone, placed in ornately carved wood frames, hung in perfect symmetry. The cove ceilings soaked up the weak light in the room reflecting it back in muted tones of yellow.

"Patricia, this is a big house. Does anyone else live here?" he asked.

"Many have come and gone in my time here, but at the moment, I am alone. I do have a man who helps me keep the place up. He fixes what needs fixing, does the yard work and brings supplies and groceries from town, but he will only come here during the day."

"Why is that?" Roland felt he knew why but wanted to hear her answer.

"He is a very superstitious man. He thinks the place is haunted. Most around here do."

Roland gave the room a tentative sweep then said, "I guess that's true of a lot of houses as old as this one."

"You're a dear," she said. "Truth is, it is a ghastly looking old house."

"If you think that, then why do you stay?"

"My family has lived in this house since my grandfather built it in 1850. I have never lived anywhere else."

Roland did some quick math in his head. He didn't know for sure, but he thought his own grandmother was born around 1940. This woman's grandfather built a house in 1850, which meant he must have been born around 1820.

"Wow," Roland said. "My family hasn't owned a piece of property for more than twenty years. My parents are now in their third house since getting married."

"That is the way of things for most," she agreed. "My grandfather made a success in lumber. That money built this house and sustained my family. Now I am all that is left of the family. Most of the money is gone now, but I don't need much, and I don't have a lot of time left. I am 120 after all."

"Patricia, if I look as good when I'm sixty as you look today, I'll count myself lucky. I think you have lots of time left."

"That's very kind of you to say, Roland, but we both know I have had more than my share of years." She patted his hand as though to acknowledge his effort to say the right thing.

"While we're on the topic, Patricia," Roland said, his demeanor changing from social to professional, "how do you explain your longevity? You've not only lived decades longer than most, but you are in spectacular condition compared to most people much younger than you."

"Oh dear," she muttered. "I feared that you would ask that question. I am, however, not sure you will believe the answer, young man."

"My job is to report the news, Patricia. Not judge it."

"I'm sure you believe that, Roland. But my tale is so fantastic that your viewers will scoff with great prejudice," she said, looking deeply into his eyes.

"Let's get the story, then we can decide how to spin it," he replied. "Okay?"

"Well," she began. "The short answer is, the reason I have lived so long is that evil never dies."

The corners of his mouth curved up into a grin. A smile born of amusement and confusion. Roland stood, looking into what, at that moment was to him, the sweetest old face he could ever remember seeing. After a moment of trying to understand what she meant, his eyes met hers, and his smile faded. Roland didn't know what he saw in her eyes, but he knew there was nothing there to smile at.

"Patricia, you are no more evil than I am. Or for that matter millions of others who have never seen eighty let alone 120," Roland said. He meant to appease her, but he may have been trying to convince himself.

"I agree that I am not evil, but I have an evil within me. The good in me, and let me be clear, I have a great deal of good inside here…" she said, tapping the fingers of her left hand over her heart, "is finally winning. That goodness has battled the evil within me for one hundred years. The good has about won that battle, and when the battle is over, I will join my family in God's house, if he will have me."

Roland paused before her, trying to make some sense of what the old woman was trying to say. He feared coming into this assignment that he would have to deal with some degree of dementia or senility. He just hoped it would be more subtle.

"Let's say for argument's sake that there is something evil inside you. How did it get there?" Something in her tone was telling Roland that this story would be worth more than the price of admission to the best stage show in Toronto.

"I think the best way to tell this story…" she said, patting his hand again, "is to get my journal. When I was a girl, I kept a journal, and although I haven't kept at it, I was quite relentless back then.

"Why don't you make yourself comfortable and I will fetch it." She left the room without waiting for a response from her guest. She moved slowly, but her stride, although agonizingly short, had an air of grace.

When the sound of her light steps faded in the distance, Roland walked over to the mantel. Lined along its length, black and white and sepia toned old pictures told stories of days gone by. People in dark suits and long dresses stood in front of horse-drawn wagons and carriages. Not a single picture appeared to Roland to have been taken after the first decade of the twentieth century.

"I see you have found my family," Patricia said as she returned to the room. Holding a large, brown leather-bound book in front of her, she looked to the collection of photos over the fireplace.

"How long have you been, as you put it, the last one left?" Roland asked, motioning to the pictures.

"The last of my family passed one hundred years ago. It's all in here," she said, stroking the spine of the journal in her hand. "Shall we get comfortable, and get to work?"

He extended his arm toward the sofa as if to usher her to her seat. She grinned, gave a quick nod and made her way to the sofa.

"Roland, dear," she said. "Before you sit, I have set out a tray with iced tea and glasses in the kitchen. Would you help an old woman and bring it in?"

She pointed to the door across the room. The door, like all the doors Roland had seen since arriving, was solid raised panel oak. This one differed slightly from the rest in that it had no knob. A tarnished brass push plate was the only hint of which way that door swung. If it hung on hinges, Roland saw no evidence of them.

"Of course," he said, striding across the room.

He gave the old door a push, and it swung open in silence.

The room on the other side was like a galley kitchen of an ocean liner from a different era. A long narrow room, lined with counters and cupboards of brilliant white. Roland released the door, and it swung back into position, stuttered a bit, then settled.

On the counter next to the door sat a silver serving tray, adorned with a large crystal pitcher of iced tea, a dish of sliced lemons, a cup of sugar, two tall glasses and serviettes.

The neatness of it made Roland smile. He was developing affection for this woman he could not explain. Normally cautious with people until getting to know them, surrendering easily to an emotional attachment to a new acquaintance did not happen to Roland Millhouse. He had few friends, and none he could say he trusted completely, but he felt something for this old woman.

He retrieved the tray and returned to his host.

Chapter 3

"It wasn't bears took that boy, I'll tell you that much," Patricia said. "He was found the next day. A terrible sight it was. Have you ever laid eyes on a dead child, Roland?"

"Only once, my cousin's boy was hit by a car when he was eleven. The whole family took it very hard."

"Well, I saw young Timmy Wilson lying in the underbrush. His eyes…" She turned away. Roland knew enough from experience with distraught people to let her be while she gathered herself. After a minute or two, she looked back to him. "His eyes," she continued. "They stared at us. We knew without having to examine him he was dead. His beautiful olive skin had turned a dull grey, and his face looked drawn as though every ounce of youth had been taken from it in the snap of a finger. His eyes…to this day, I wake seeing Timmy's eyes, looking at those eyes looking back at me." Her head was shaking slowly, as if she hoped the gesture could stop the boy's gaze from seeing her.

"Were they able to determine the cause of death?" Roland asked.

"That's the funny thing," she said. "Doctor McKinney said the boy had been all but drained. Not a drop of blood left in his little body. Now, I have lived my whole life here, Roland, and back a hundred years ago bears managed to kill a few citizens. Especially in the spring when they were starved from the winter hibernation, but a bear never did that."

"I'm sorry to be insensitive, Patricia, but how is this relevant to your longevity?" He hoped the impatience he was feeling didn't come through in his voice.

"Evil," she whispered. "Evil is what killed the boy." She tapped her index finger to her heart again. "That same evil lives in here."

Roland's lips curved up slightly, in spite of his greatest effort not to show his amusement. Patricia had already let him know that she didn't have time for skeptics. If he decided to hear the rest of the story, after she finished her explanation of the evil within, then he had to keep his attitude in check.

"I know, you young people today only believe what you see and if you don't want to hear this story then tell me now. Because, dear, it's a long story and if I don't tell you the whole thing, without skipping any of it, you'll leave here thinking a crazy old woman wasted your whole day."

Patricia looked into his eyes. The smile had left his lips, but more importantly, it was gone from his eyes.

"Well?" she said, studying his reaction.

He gave her a nod of agreement and said, "I am terribly sorry, Patricia.

Please continue."

Patricia's Journal—Monday, April 15, 1912

Daddy is still not home. Oh, I do wish he would come back, but he isn't due for another week.

Timmy Wilson's funeral was today. The whole town attended. Even that sour Mrs. Murtry from the general store. Timmy looked like he was sleeping in that coffin, and I wanted to stop them when they closed the lid. He didn't look dead the way he did in the woods.

After the funeral, Pete Laurier from the telegraph office rushed to tell us some big ship sank in the north sea, and hundreds were dead. We were sad to hear it, but mostly I was sad about young Timmy.

"Titanic?" Roland asked.

She nodded. "Dreadful that was. All those poor people freezing to death in that cold water."

"Arrogance is mankind's deadliest trait," he said.

Patricia nodded, but the Titanic wasn't what she wanted to discuss.

"You couldn't believe how Timmy Wilson looked in that coffin. He was still pale, sure. His face still hollow but his color had come back some, and his skin had, I don't know. Relaxed? Yes, it had relaxed.'

Roland lifted the pitcher of iced tea, his hand steady as he poured her a glass, the ice cubes clinking as they fell in. He placed the glass in her hand, folding her fingers around it, and held them in place until he was sure her grip was firm.

"You're sweet, Roland," she said.

He poured himself a glass, and they drank in silence. Him in big gulps and Patricia with sips so delicate it seemed she would not ever finish.

"Roland, would you mind if we walked some? It is a lovely day."

Chapter 4

Shuffling alongside Patricia to the front walk, Roland anticipated a five-minute stroll around the yard. She may not have looked her age, but how far could a person that old walk? To his surprise, Patricia led him the length of the driveway and out to the road.

"Where are we going?" he asked.

"There is something I think you need to see. Are you okay to walk, Roland?"

He couldn't help but laugh. This tiny ancient person was sincere in her concern that he may not be up for a slow stroll through the country.

"Yes, I was worried about you," he said.

"You needn't be. I have been walking this same path near every day for a hundred years."

She pointed to his left. "Over there is the steeple of St. Thomas's. It isn't the same bell that rang the morning we went looking for Timmy. That summer the church burned to the ground along with a great deal of the town. But they rebuilt it as if from a picture. If I hadn't told you, you would never know."

"Do they still use it as a distress signal?" he asked.

"No, with television and radio, and all them people with phones that do near everything but make your dinner, there isn't a need to use a church bell. Now it only rings on Sunday morning."

"It must have been a comfort to the people of the town to have the church back the way it was," he said.

Patricia shrugged, then pointed down the slope to her right. "About a mile that way is where we found Timmy. Most of the trees are gone now, but this whole area was thick forest back then."

It was slow going. Roland found himself stopping every third stride to let Patricia keep up. If she noticed, she didn't seem to care.

After about twenty minutes, Patricia made her way to a bench in the grass at the side of the road. She sat with the same grace she did every-thing. Roland marveled at the fluidity of her every motion, still unable to believe she was so old. She let out a slight "whoosh" when she settled on the bench and patted the seat next to her.

Her cheeks looked flushed a bit, but as far as Roland could tell, she was not out of breath nor fatigued from the walk.

"I had the bench put here about ten years ago. I was starting to get tired on my walks. I decided I was getting too old."

Roland hadn't noticed Patricia carrying the journal until she sat on the bench and placed it in her lap. Now she brushed the cover as if trying to smooth out the pages inside.

She didn't say anything, just sat looking out across the field that bor-dered the opposite side of the road. Roland looked in that direction but saw nothing that might hold her attention. He took two steps to the bench and sat beside her.

She flipped open the cover and turned to the page marked with a rib-bon. Running her palm over the words as though trying to conjure spirits from her past, her gaze returned to the field across the road for a moment, then she read aloud.

Patricia's Journal—Tuesday, April 16, 1912

I walked to town with Mother this morning. She was quite melan-choly. Partly because she misses Daddy, but I think she is frightened by what happened to Timmy.

Mrs. Scully was in the common, so we went to say hello. That's when we found out that Mr. Wilson was missing and Mrs. Wilson has taken to her bed in grief.

She started telling Mother about that ship that sank, but Mother just excused us and spirited us home.

I really wish Daddy were home.

Mother is so scared.

Patricia closed the book, again running her hand over it like she might be petting a cat or small dog. Without warning, she stood and motioned for Roland to join her. He stood beside her, and they continued to walk. The click of Roland's Italian shoes on the pavement and the breeze rustling the tall grass at the edge of the road made the only sound.

"They found Mr. Wilson the next day," she said, breaking the silence. "Most people were saying he was overcome with sadness and ran off."

"Mother said they were wrong. He was so fond of that boy, and Mrs. Wilson too. They told Mother that Mr. Wilson looked the same way as Timmy. The townfolk said it was some strange sickness, and likely Mrs. Wilson would be next. Nobody would go over to the Wilson place to check on the poor woman."

Being the true gentleman Roland considered himself to be, he said, "Patricia, let me carry that for you." He reached for the journal. She released it without protest, and he tucked it under his arm.

"Was she next?" he asked.

"Not next, but it did get her. It got many of them."

"What did? Was it a plague, or some epidemic?"

"It was evil, plain and simple. Do you remember what I told you about evil, Roland?"

"It never dies," he said in a whisper. He wasn't buying into her tale completely, but she was definitely creeping him out.

CHAPTER 5

They walked in silence for a while, open field on their left and a row of tall cedars on the right. A gap in the trees revealed the Kings Shore Cemetery. Patricia walked to a stone bench just inside the gate.

"Roland, I want you to walk around and have a look. Come back when you're finished, and we'll go back for another glass of tea."

"What am I looking for?" he asked.

"Dear, if you don't find it, maybe you aren't made out for this reporter business," she said, grinning up at him.

He returned the journal to her waiting hands, smiled back, then turned and walked among the headstones. He took a pad and pen from his breast pocket. He didn't know why until he got to the Wilson grave. Timmy, April 12. Thomas, April 16. Myra, April 21. The biggest marker read Owens, Robert, June 6 and Louise, June 9. Patricia's parents. He didn't know for sure, but he was fairly certain.

"Jesus," he said under his breath. Then he looked next at the Bergeron marker. Bergeron, John, April 16 and Jennifer, April 17. All of them in 1912.

So it went. Roland found forty-three headstones dated April through June of 1912. He shuffled back to the bench where his host still sat. His swagger had drained; somehow he felt aged. He dropped onto the bench beside her, his hands on his knees to keep him upright. This whole time he wanted to write this story off as the ramblings of a lonely old woman seeking attention. Although the headstones didn't prove anything evil, Roland was starting to believe in Patricia Owens.

"What happened to them?"

"It was like a wagon rolling down a hill, once it gets to moving, it either has to coast to a stop at the bottom or crash," she said. "In Kings Shore in 1912, the wagon made it to the bottom, but it crashed anyway. Do you understand that, Roland?"

"I understand that some God-awful event took place here. What it was or what stopped it is a mystery to me."

"God-awful. That's about right. God-awful." The last one she dragged out, giving her a southern hillbilly tone.

She opened the book to where she last placed her ribbon.

Patricia's Journal—Saturday, April 20, 1912

Constable Morgan dropped by today. He said he knew Daddy was not home and he wanted to make sure we were fine.

Mother thanked him and told him that our hand was here, but his thoughtfulness was accepted with gratitude.

Mother didn't know I was listening through the door. Constable Morgan told her that Sam Pierce is going around telling people he saw Mr. Wilson last night.

What a mean thing to say, with Mrs. Wilson grieving so.

"I can see the doubt in your eyes, Roland," she said. "Before you set your mind firm against what you are hearing, I ask you to please, hear it all. Can you do that?"

Roland stared off into the distance while he did the math in his head. "Patricia," he said in a tone that indicated he just found a hole in her story big enough to drive a truck through. "Wilson died on the…" he flipped open his pad. "Sixteenth, that entry was dated the…"

"Twentieth," Patricia interrupted. "Four nights after he died, Sam Pierce, who until that day was considered a good man in Kings Shore, one of the most reliable, claimed he saw Tom Wilson walking along the road toward his farm."

"Did he speak to him? Sam, I mean. Did he speak to the guy? The man he claimed to be Tom Wilson."

"If you saw a man you knew to be dead and buried walking down a deserted road at night, would you try to strike up a conversation, Roland?" Her answer was so acute, it seemed almost scripted. It was plain to Roland that Patricia expected him to ask the question.

"I suppose not," he answered. "I didn't see Sam Pierce's name in the graveyard." It wasn't a question, but Patricia answered it anyway.

"That's because he isn't there. He packed his belongings into a wagon and left before the end of the week. He was one of the smart ones. He may have lost his home and his friends, but he kept his life."

"Did anyone else leave?" Roland asked.

"It was a small town, and most didn't have much, but what they had was here, so they stayed. Mother and I couldn't leave. We had to wait for Daddy to get back. I wished so that he would come home. I wished it so much, and by the time he did, I wished he had not."

She stood, and began to walk back toward the house. Roland followed in silence. This was Patricia's dance, and he was content to let her lead. She held the book to her bosom, and this time Roland chose not to offer to carry it. She held it to her like a child holding a doll. If the book gave her comfort, then good on her. They walked without talking until the old woman sat on her bench. Not at all leg weary, Roland found himself silently thanking the person who installed this bench. His mind was trying to process a great deal, and he found the experience taxing.

"Do you know why I put this bench in this spot, Roland?" she asked, placing the journal on the bench beside her.

"I figured it was halfway," he said.

"No," she said. "We're much closer to the cemetery than we are the house."

"I couldn't even offer a guess then."

She pointed to a barely noticeable path directly across the road. He turned, squinting into the shadows of the tall grass and trees along the path.

"What is down there?" he asked.

"It's better if you just go see. Along that path, you will see the ruins of an old farmhouse. It's not much more than a stone foundation now. It's about five hundred yards in. Another hundred yards or so beyond that is the remains of a silo. Was a barn too but it's long gone. Just behind that is a big rock. You can't miss it. It's near as big as a VW."

"What's special about a rock in the middle of a long-gone farm?" He looked at her, but Patricia just stared down the path.

Without saying another word, Roland stood, and after making sure the way was clear, he crossed the road. At the mouth of the path leading into the shadows, he turned back to the bench. Patricia just shooed him away as though he were a bothersome child. With a shake of his head, unable to believe what the old lady had convinced him to do, he stepped along the path.

Chapter 6

One mosquito bite on the back of his neck told Roland he had had enough of this. The old lady was a master of intrigue. She would draw him in, then set him adrift. Draw him in and set him adrift.

When she had his attention, she owned him. Then he would come to his senses, like now, and want nothing more than to get back on the road to Toronto. Yet he didn't. He followed her directions, swatting at bugs, and cursing the brambles that tugged at his trousers.

The stone foundation rose up from the grass just as Patricia described it. He scanned the area behind what was once a house, and hiding half behind a sickly pine was the rubble from a long-destroyed silo. He struggled his way through the shrubbery, grass, and weeds.

When he got to within fifty feet of the silo, he saw the rock. As Patricia said, it was the size of a VW. It wasn't the size or shape, or even wondering how the big rock got there that captured Roland's curiosity. It was the surrounding dirt.

The rock, stark and white, surrounded by a ring of black, barren dirt, looked like a pearl in a black oyster. Nothing grew in that ring of soil, not grass, nor weeds or even moss. By contrast, the white VW-sized rock looked almost luminous in the middle of the dull black ring.

Mesmerized by the oddness of it, Roland inched closer, his steps tentative. A chill ran through him as his foot touched the dead ground. Make no mistake, the ground encircling that rock did not support life of any kind.

Sweat dripped from his face. A few drops fell to the dirt making even blacker spots on the surface. In seconds the moist spots billowed up from the ground in tiny puffs of vapor. Roland crouched at the line where the grass ended and the barren circle began. He held his hand over it, and goosebumps erupted from his hand, up his arm, to his neck.

A shiver ran through him, and he lost his balance. Roland placed his hand on the dirt to steady himself. Immediately he cringed as his abdomen clenched and a gorge of nasty erupted from his mouth. A puddle of hot vomit stained the ground, and the smell rising in a cloud of putrid mist caused him to retch again.

His muscles twitched, and he couldn't stop shivering. Roland pushed himself away from the rock. He spun on his butt and rose to his knees. He remained there on all fours, waiting to see if he would vomit again.

After a minute or two, he stood and began to jog back to the road. His gait was staggered, but he kept running. The farther from the rock he ran, the stronger he felt and the faster his strides came.

When he got to the bench, Patricia was sitting with the book in her lap and her hands folded neatly on the cover. An O.P.P. cruiser pulled to a stop beside them.

"Is everything okay, Miss Owens?" the officer called over from the driver's side.

Roland collapsed on the bench next to Patricia. His chest heaved as he took huge gulps of air to feed his burning lungs. Sweat ran down his face in torrents, and his shirt was wet under the arms, and along his back and chest.

"Everything is as good as it can be, Jimmy," she replied. "This here is Roland Millhouse. He is a reporter, here from Toronto. He came to wish me a happy birthday. Isn't that nice?"

Patricia patted Roland's leg and smiled at Officer Jimmy. When the black and white Crown Vic disappeared up the road, Roland's gaze went from the car to the old woman on the bench next to him.

"Wha…wha…wha…" He took a few deep breaths and tried again.

"What was that?"

"It's the evil," she said. "I told you, evil never dies."

"I touched the ground," he said. His eyes were wide with fear. "I felt, I felt like…"

"I think, Roland, that you have no idea what you felt like," she said. "I doubt you have ever felt anything like that."

"It made me physically ill," he said, wiping a tear from his cheek. "I threw up when my hand touched the ground over there."

"Let's go back to the house," she said. "I think we can both use a glass of iced tea."

Chapter 7

They walked along without saying a word. Roland didn't have to adjust his stride or effort to accommodate the centenarian's diminished stride. His own feet were dragging, his pricey leather shoes looked like rejects from a rummage sale as he scuffed his feet through the gravel at the edge of the blacktop.

Patricia let him be for a while. She knew that sooner was better than later to try to give him an explanation. She would have to make him understand, at least as much as she understood what he had just experienced.

"It isn't known for sure what is down there," she said. "I can only relay what I overheard. One of the old men in town told this story to my father."

Roland said nothing, just nodded and continued to shuffle his feet toward Patricia's house. His color was returning and the stoop in his shoulders had gone, but he remained silent.

"It began back in 1872," she said. "Kings Shore was not much more than an outpost for the fur trade, but a few families had settled here."

She looked at him and immediately felt uncertain about continuing. His face dripped with sweat; his shoulders slumped again as though the mere suggestion of what he felt at the rock had caused a relapse. He shuffled onward toward the old mansion with the posture of an old man, and his stride was again unsteady and staggered.

"Are you sure you are well enough to hear this, Roland?" she asked.

He nodded but remained silent.

Patricia took his elbow in her left hand while her right continued to caress her journal.

"In 1872, children started to disappear. Girls, every one of them was a girl, most between ten and thirteen, some from Kings Shore and some from what is now called Sauble Beach and the surrounding area between here and there.

"I can see you're not much in the mood for talking but I would appreciate it if you would just let me tell you what the old man told my father without asking any questions. Can you do that, Roland?" Another nod.

"Good! I have had nightmares about this story so many times through my years. I can almost recite it just as that man told it. That is what I will try to do, but I would rather tell it straight through. The man who told it was a coward, but he told the girl's family where she was, the girl in the story I am about to tell you. While the child's father and uncle and the others gathered, this man rushed out like he was going to help, but he didn't help. He cowered in the shadows of the woods watching. The girl would not have been saved if the others arrived just minutes later than they did. The man would have hid there, and watched."

Patricia walked on for a while without speaking. She made it seem like she needed to catch her breath, but really she was stalling. She didn't fear much after what she'd lived through, but she feared this story.

"This is, in his words, what the old man told my father. ."

Terror doesn't belong on a pretty face, certainly not on the face of young Winifred Samuels. In the moonlight, Winnie's eyes seemed preternaturally large. Her golden hair, surely neatly braided when she left for school that morning, hung behind each ear like two frazzled ropes. The girl balanced on a rough-cut plank stretched across an open stone well, her arms bound at the wrists and pulled taut above her head by a rope tied off on an overhanging limb of a sugar maple.

Her shoulders must have ached from the strain, and her thighs quivered as the terrified child struggled to maintain her balance. Small for her age and fragile from repeated bouts of all manner of illness, Winnie looked much younger than her thirteen years. Tears streamed down her cheeks, and her body shuddered with uncontrollable weeping.

Malachi Adams admired the beauty and purity of the child. Excited by the vision before him, his breathing quickened to match the rapid heaving of Winnie's naked torso. Most would think the girl diseased as the moon's glow seeped through the trees leaving blotches of shadow on her pale skin.

"You are the prettiest one yet," Malachi told her.

Winnie didn't reply. The only sounds she made came in barely audible whimpers and the fast rhythmic rush of her breathing. The girl looked down on him, not speaking, but her eyes conveyed her thoughts more clearly than words ever could.

Please don't hurt me. I want to go home. Daddy, save me.

"You will be number thirteen," Malachi told her. "After the blood of thirteen virgins has been spilled in the circle, a succubus will come to me. She will be enslaved by me, and do as I bid. So you see, child, you should be honored."

He stepped over the circle of salt running around the well, dropped his robe and stood naked before the girl, his body as hairless as a newborn.

Winnie squeezed her eyes shut. Her crying came in loud gasps. Her small frame convulsed with the effort to stop.

"I know this is very frightening," Malachi said in a soothing voice. "But you are here to become a part of a greater existence than you can comprehend."

At the base of the well, Malachi opened a wooden box and retrieved a silver dagger. The ivory handle absorbed the moonlight, becoming luminescent. Winnie opened her eyes at the sound of the complaining hinges of the box. The sight of the gleaming double-edged blade was too much for her. From her very soul, the girl screamed for her mother and her father.

"Child, child," Malachi said, trying to soothe her. "No one can hear you."

Winnie stopped screaming, but her sobs came steady and her small body jerked with each breath. The plank beneath her feet wobbled violently.

"Succubus," Malachi called, his face looking up to the sky. "Tonight I shall bathe in the blood of the thirteenth virgin sacrificed in your name."

He stepped up to the edge of the well and lightly traced a line down the length of Winnie's thigh. Her screams filled the air. Seconds later Winnie's pleas were replaced by a thunderous report to Malachi's left. He dropped the dagger as a musket-ball struck his shoulder.

The smell of spent gunpowder filled the air. Five men appeared from the darkness of the trees. Amos Smith, a stout man in the middle of the pack took charge immediately.

"Demon," Amos shouted at Malachi. Malachi made no attempt to escape. He looked at those men, with contempt.

Desmond Samuals called to his daughter, "Winnie, are you unharmed?"

"Desmond," said Amos. "Take your little girl home."

"Daddy, Daddy," the child cried as Desmond rushed to her, removing his shirt.

He gingerly untied her hands, then covered his daughter with the shirt. Winnie wrapped her arms around her father's neck, and he carried her into the woods.

"John," Amos said. "The child is your niece, see to it your brother gets her home." With that, John followed Desmond and Winnie into the trees.

Blood streamed through the fingers of Malachi's left hand as he tried to staunch the gush. He stared in confused wonder, first at his shoulder, then at the three men before him. Fear hadn't left the circle when Desmond carried his baby girl away, it just changed vessels. Malachi Adams, naked and bleeding, fell to his knees, and all three men looked down at fear. Malachi was not afraid. Malachi was fear. He looked up at his captors with defiant indifference.

"The walls around that house of evil won't protect you here, Malachi

Adams," Amos said.

Malachi looked up into his accusers' faces with a nonchalance that bordered on boredom. It was almost like he didn't feel these men were worthy of his full attention.

"Drop him in the well," Amos yelled. Some of the bravado had left his face, replaced by fear of the bleeding man at his feet.

They seized Malachi by the arms. He didn't resist, or plead for his life. Malachi was calm. Malachi himself would be the thirteenth virgin sacrificed. He didn't cry out in pain as they pulled him across the grass to the base of the well, his wounded shoulder tugged and twisted with the effort. The well gaped open in the moonlight like the very mouth of Satan awaiting a tasty morsel. Malachi didn't make a sound as his body fell through the blackness to what was surely death. He just disappeared.

Amos Smith and his companions stood before the mouth of the open well. They looked to each other for a sign that what they had just done was right. Without making eye contact, they seemed to agree. It was the only thing they could do.

All three men then looked to the edge of the well, but none had dared to look down into the black chasm. None had the nerve to look down on the evil they had just cast to the blackness of the earth for fear evil would jump up and pull them down with it.

"Tomorrow bring a team of horses up here and drag that rock over top of the hole," said Amos, motioning to a large boulder ten yards away.

"It'll take a team of four, maybe six," one of the men said.

"Then bring eight," replied Amos.

Patricia released Roland's elbow, clung to her journal and hugged it to her bosom.

"The man who told Daddy this story crept over to the well. He didn't look down to the blackness, but he said he heard Malachi Adams laughing."

Chapter 8

Roland had recovered some as they walked, and he listened.

"So you're telling me that that is the rock, and there is a dead serial killer at the bottom of a well beneath it?" he said, breaking his silence.

"That is the rock. And beneath the rock is what was a well More than likely it has all filled in by now. As memory serves, that rock used to sit much higher when I was young."

"And it's been there since that night?" he asked.

"If only that were true," she replied, shaking her head. "If only it were."

"What do you mean?"

"As it turns out a family of squatters came to town. That was quite common back then. They happened on the abandoned home of Malachi Adams and moved in. This was in 1911, just before the first frost. Name was Steen, Ben and Gloria and a little girl named Lizzy. Nice couple, the Steens, but they mostly kept to themselves, and nobody thought to mention what was beneath that rock. I guess they couldn't imagine anybody moving it. But, somehow they did move it.

Mr. Steen saw it for what it was. A covered well. Turns out it was dry as a bone."

"Dry as a whole skeleton, more like it," Roland whispered.

"The girl, Lizzy, fell in that hellhole. Poor thing split her head open on the rocks down there. Bled to death before Mr. Steen could lower himself down with a rope."

"Jesus," Roland said. "Did he find…"

"The only thing he found down there was his little girl. Her broken body lying on the blood-stained stones at the bottom of a black hole."

"But how?"

"Well, to begin with, everyone who lived around there in '72, was by this time either dead or moved away. Everyone had gone except that cowardly old man, the man who told that awful story to my father. So, you see, the whole Malachi Adams story was more folklore than history. Not the kind of thing a town wants to remember. Not the kind of story they tell new residents."

"So it was just a story that old man made up?" Roland asked.

"Roland, why do you think they would have covered the well with a rock that big?"

He pondered this question for a moment. "It went dry, and they covered it so little girls didn't fall in."

"Yes," she said. "That is a possibility. But, surely they would have just filled it in with field stones and dirt. Or, as was the practice back then, carpentered from planks a cover for it.

"Do you remember me saying the girl was lying on the blood-stained rocks?"

He nodded.

"The rocks were stained, but there was no blood." She looked at him to see if this was sinking in. "The girl bled to death down there. Her father got there minutes later. The rocks were red, but the blood was gone."

"Are you trying to tell me that Malachi Adams waited, buried alive for what? Forty years, then lapped up that girl's blood?"

"I am not trying to tell you anything, yet."

They had gotten to the driveway where Roland's Bimmer gleamed in the late afternoon sun. She saw him looking at it longingly, as they made their way toward the house.

"It's a bit late to head back to Toronto, Roland. If you want to stay,

I have plenty of spare rooms. If you are convinced I'm as mad as a rabid dog and would rather be on your way, I would recommend you drop in on the Twin Oaks B&B. You've had quite a long day."

"Thank you for your time, and sharing your story, Patricia," he said. "The B&B sounds like a good idea. Can I stop in tomorrow before I leave?"

"Of course, Roland. You must know that I have only told you a small part of the story. I hope you can find some time in the morning to hear more before you leave."

"We shall see," he said.

Roland left Patricia standing on the porch. He fully intended to return to Toronto. He would do a fluff piece about the nice old lady. Include a picture of her standing on the porch, and hope his next assignment would get him attention from the right people.

What Roland hadn't anticipated was the pull of the evil. He had to pass by the path that led him to the VW-sized rock. When he got there, he pulled over to the side of the road and stopped. He didn't plan it. He couldn't even say he did it intentionally, yet there he was, staring along the path toward that evil place as the sun fell below the horizon. It was almost as though the thing called to him and he was powerless to resist.

Roland reached for the handle to open the door, and just as he was about to push the door open, a pickup buzzed by, horn blazing. Roland recoiled from the sudden noise, put the car in gear, checked for more cars, then slowly guided the Bimmer back onto the road. He watched the path disappear behind him, then resumed a comfortable 60 k/h.

Roland's heart was pounding, and he realized Patricia was right. He had a long, tough day and the B&B was a good idea.

Chapter 9

Dressed in slacks and a short-sleeved blouse, Patricia opened the door moments after the bell rang.

"I didn't expect to see you again young man," she said.

Roland gave her a shy grin. "To tell you the truth, I didn't expect to be back."

"What changed your mind?"

"A couple of things," he said. "First thing, I left my camera in your parlor." They both shared a chuckle.

"By the look of your casual attire this morning, you do plan to be driving back to the city," she said, motioning to his tan chinos and navy polo shirt.

He shuffled his canvas deck shoes on the porch boards and worked on his nonchalant posture.

"You said there was two things that brought you back."

"The evil," he said. "Last night when I left, I stopped where the path goes down from the road. I don't even remember stopping the car. If it wasn't for a truck horn, I may have gone back down there. Something tells me that would have been a bad idea."

"Have you had breakfast, Roland?" she asked.

"I was just going to grab a coffee at Tim Horton's, and get lunch on the road."

She stepped to the side, still holding the door open. Roland entered the house and followed her into the kitchen.

"I was just about to have some fruit and a cup of tea," she said. "Would you like some?"

"That would be fine, but what I would really like is to hear the rest of your story."

Patricia set a bowl of fruit salad in front of him. She retrieved a cup and saucer from the cupboard and set it next to the fruit. She filled his cup from the teapot and left the room.

Roland marveled at the serving tray on the table. A small dish of lemon wedges, a bowl of sugar, a stack of cookies and a tiny honey pot surrounded the teapot.

He squeezed a lemon wedge into his cup, then added a teaspoon of honey. After a small sip to taste, he added another spoonful of honey.

He nibbled a cookie when Patricia returned carrying the journal. The book looked older and somehow more ominous to her young guest. Roland watched the book as if it had a life of its own. As if it might be dangerous.

She must have noticed his unease. "It is only a book, dear."

He gave her a nervous smile, then asked, "Patricia, before you continue telling me any more. Why now? You have kept this to yourself for one hundred years. Why have you decided to tell the story now? And, why me?"

"As I mentioned, Roland, I am not going to live forever. I dearly hope that all you get from me is a fantastic story. What I fear is that what happened all those years ago can happen again. If it does, the things I am about to tell you may save the lives of many if you give heed to my words."

"It sounds like a great weight to burden one man with," Roland said.

"That is one of the reasons I chose you. You just might be able to get the message to many. Maybe it will be on the television, or maybe it will be some other way, but with your job, I hope you will find a way to share my story. She set the journal on the table and sat across from Roland.

She sipped her tea and began to eat her fruit. The sun washed the room in a comforting light.

Roland kept the conversation going by explaining his evening in the B&B. She smiled while he told her about his dinner at the café, and his walk around the town common.

"The town common is a lovely place," she said. "It still looks as it did when I was a girl. Everything but that dreadful-looking playground equipment anyway. Damn thing looks like a giant spider web, but the children love climbing around on it."

Patricia opened the journal to the page marked by the ribbon.

Patricia's Journal—Sunday, April 21, 1912

I went to see Mrs. Wilson today. Mother forbade me from going, so I told her I was going to Penelope's to see her engagement ring.

She knew I was excited to see Penelope's ring, so she didn't question me further.

Poor Mrs. Wilson looked terrible sick. And she was talking nonsense. She insisted that Timmy was coming back to see her tonight. That he came last night and hugged her so tight she thought she would faint.

Poor Mrs. Wilson.

Penelope's ring is stunning.

"Mrs. Wilson wasn't making it up," Patricia said. "I thought she really believed her boy had come to visit her. The mind can play tricks when you're in grief, and her grief was double. I couldn't tell anyone, however. If I did, Mother would know I went against her wishes. I wasn't a child, but I still minded my mother."

"Did you go back?"

"I did. The very next day." She fiddled with the ribbon.

Roland watched as she slid it between her fingers. She had such delicate hands. Not the gnarled, bony talons you'd expect on a woman so old.

"Mrs. Wilson was barely alive when I got there. I couldn't leave her another day. I went directly to town and got the doctor. Fool man didn't want to go out to the Wilsons. I told him if he didn't I would surely send

Daddy to give him a talking to when he came home. Daddy was something of a big deal around here, so the doctor hitched his buggy, and I went with him back to see Mrs. Wilson.

"That fool man didn't say a word to me the whole way out to the Wilsons place. Treated me like I was some mischievous school girl. But I didn't need to be a doctor to read the doctor's face when he laid eyes on poor Mrs. Wilson."

"Did he say what was wrong with her?" Roland asked.

"No, just barked out orders, like I was his assistant. Get some water, fetch the woman another blanket, open that window."

Patricia poured herself another cup of tea, added a spoonful of honey, and raised her cup toward Roland. He declined another cup with a shake of his head.

"When I slid those curtains open, well, poor Mrs. Wilson screamed like the devil himself was shining through that glass. Dr. McKinney yelled to close the curtains, like I took it upon myself to open them.

"As soon as I closed the curtains, she settled down. My heart pounded so hard I thought it was going to explode from my chest. Her scream scared me so."

"Was there anything out there?" he asked.

"If there were, it would have to be a bird. Mrs. Wilson slept upstairs. Wasn't nothing coming near that window but glorious sunshine. It was a brilliant day, a bit cool, but the sun was so warm.

"Dr. McKinney sent me to fetch help. Said to bring somebody who could help me bring Mrs. Wilson down the stairs to the buggy. He planned to take her to his house so he could watch over her. I didn't think he was such an ass after he told me that."

Patricia covered a smile with her hand. At 120, she still felt awkward about using colorful language.

CHAPTER 10

Patricia stood and gathered the dishes. Roland followed her lead. Five minutes later, they sat on wicker chairs on the veranda facing the western sky. The sun was high in the sky, but they were still well-shaded beneath the overhang. The morning dew had long since evaporated, joining the wispy clouds high in the atmosphere.

"Did Mrs. Wilson get to the doctor's place okay?" Roland asked. He no longer asked questions like a reporter after a story. He asked them like a child hearing a riveting fairy tale, wide-eyed and his attention devoted to her words.

"Well, dear," she said. "She did get there alive. Was she okay? No, I don't think you could say that.

"That poor lady looked a dreadful sight. Her eyes looked like holes in her skull, and her skin looked as grey as the face of her dead child the day they found him in the woods.

"Roland," Patricia said, placing her hand on his, "when they got her out of bed, she was so thin. Her pink nightgown hung on her like a blanket on a clothesline. She was half the woman she had been just days before.

"She wasn't strong enough to get out of bed, but she had plenty of strength to argue with the men who helped get her to the buggy." Patricia giggled when she recalled the memory. "Some of the words I heard her use, I'd never heard spoken by a woman until that day. She insisted that if she left, Timmy would not know where to find her. Of course, Dr. McKinney just thought these the ramblings of a delirious woman."

"You didn't believe that though, did you, Patricia?"

"It was in her eyes. There was nothing in her eyes but concern for her boy. Sure, she was concerned about a child who was in the ground, but somehow her eyes told me that Timmy would be back to find her. It was those eyes that kept me from sleep that spring and summer. When someone made a comment about the impossible, I saw Mrs. Wilson's eyes. I saw the knowledge that not everything we know to be true is in fact true. Does that make any sense to you?"

"I think so," Roland said. "There is a whole lot of world out there. Mankind will be discovering new things centuries after we are all gone. Things that people of today think impossible."

"Something like that," she said. "Something very much like that."

The sun had crept around to the side of the house, and the far end of the veranda was now soaking in the brilliant spring sunshine. A grey tabby leaped up on the railing, stretched out, dug its claws into the ancient wood, then went to sleep.

"Yours?" Roland asked, motioning to the now sleeping feline.

"Do you have a cat, Roland?"

"A pet rock would die at my house, Patricia. I am never home." They both snickered at that. More than was probably called for.

"No, Scuba isn't mine. I don't think anyone can own a cat, Roland. Cats belong only to themselves. They only do the bidding of people if it suits their own agenda. Wouldn't you agree?"

His lips curved up in a grin that made it all the way to his eyes. "His name is Scuba?"

"Oh, that's what I call him. If he visits anybody else around here, I'm sure he is called something completely different."

"Why Scuba?" he asked, the grin still in place.

"Why not? Look at him. Can you think of a better name?"

He said nothing, just shrugged and looked back to Scuba, as if the cat might tell him.

"What happened to Mrs. Wilson?" he asked after he lost interest in Scuba.

"They got Mrs. Wilson downstairs easy enough. While the men helped her down the stairs, Dr. McKinney instructed me to open the door. Roland, when she saw the sunlight spilled into the room, she shrieked like she had been set afire.

"The doctor yelled at me to shut the door, once again like I opened it of my own accord, when all along whose instructions did I follow?"

Roland didn't answer, and she didn't look to him for one.

"While they were trying to soothe her, I ran to her room and fetched her blanket. It was macabre watching them wrap a living woman up like that, but what else could they do?"

Patricia began to giggle when she pondered what she would say next.

"Those men were not loggers, and by the time that they carried Mrs. Wilson to the buggy and wrestled her onto the seat, they were spent. Huffing and puffing like overworked plough-horses.

"She made it to Dr. McKinney's well enough, such as she was. The doctor's guest room was on the second floor, and the men had it much harder getting her up, as you might imagine.

"Before long, Mrs. McKinney had her all tucked in. The doctor told his wife to get her some broth and water. 'Try to keep her drinking,' Dr. McKinney said.

She was anemic and needed lots of fluid to get her blood up.

"That's as much as I can tell you first hand on that," Patricia said. "Dr. McKinney thanked me for my assistance and sent me home. Dismissed me like I was a child."

"I saw her name on one of those headstones. She died that spring. She didn't get better at the McKinneys', did she?" Roland was so deep into this story now that he would have passed on an interview with Elvis, found alive and well and living in Kalamazoo, if it meant leaving before hearing the rest.

Patricia picked up the journal from the table next to her chair. Roland didn't remember seeing her bring it out, but it was there. She opened it, set the ribbon on her lap, and ran her hand over the page.

Patricia's Journal—Tuesday, April 23, 1912

I went to see Mrs. Wilson at Dr. McKinney's today. Mrs. McKinney told me Mrs. Wilson was doing better, but she was resting and couldn't have visitors.

When I tried to leave, she told me to sit a moment.

I wish I hadn't. Mrs. McKinney told me something terrible. She went to check on Mrs. Wilson before going to bed herself and she saw something in the window. It was Timmy, clinging to the window ledge, peering into the room.

She screamed so loud it strained her voice. She still sounded like a woman on the tail end of laryngitis. Dr. McKinney come running up to see what was wrong, and he could only say, "Dear Lord."

They both ran out to the side of the house to help the boy down from there, and that was when they knew something in Kings Shore was very wrong.

Timmy Wilson hissed at them like a feral cat might, then scurried down the side of the house like a spider.

"The dead kid climbed up the side of a house to a second-story window? Why didn't he climb in?" Roland asked, with more than a hint of skepticism.

"Be careful, young man. This story gets much more fantastic. If you are not in this for the whole ride, you might as well drive back to Toronto."

"I'm sorry, Patricia. But you have to know how this sounds."

"Why do you think the story has gone untold for one hundred years?"

"Can I ask you why you are telling it now?"

"You can, and I believe you did," she answered. "I am going to die soon, Roland." She held a hand up to staunch his protest. "My body has played host to a battle for so very long. Good vs. evil. Well, the evil has been all but cast out, and now I am free. Free to join Mother and Daddy."

Chapter 11

When the sun flooded over the rest of the veranda, Patricia led her guest inside. They settled in the parlor. Roland squinted through the darkness as his eyes adjusted to the gloom inside Patricia's favorite room. The shades were drawn, and the curtains closed tight, letting in only enough light to brighten the outer fringes of the fabric. A wind chime somewhere outside ushered in a sound so innocent, it seemed foreign inside these darkened rooms.

"Would you like me to let in some light?" Roland asked.

"I like to keep them closed in the afternoon," Patricia said. "The house stays cooler. I had air conditioning put in some years back, but I just don't like the way it makes the air feel. Do you know what I mean?"

"My mother says the same thing. She likes the cool air, but she rarely runs her air conditioner, unless it is over eighty-five."

Patricia nodded then motioned to the kitchen. "Be a dear, and get us some cool drinks."

Without a word, he went through the same door he had yesterday. On the counter, he found a tray with two glasses, a dish of sugar and a bowl of peanuts. He looked in the fridge and found a pitcher filled with what surely was lemonade.

"There is a bowl of ice in the freezer," Patricia called from the other room.

Grinning, he opened the freezer door. He retrieved the pitcher, added the ice, placed it on the tray and returned to his host. He found her seated with the journal in her lap.

"You were that sure I would come back today?" he asked, holding the tray up for effect.

"I had an inkling." She had a way of saying so much without saying anything. Her eyes spoke volumes that her lips never had to verbalize.

He set the tray on the coffee table, poured two glasses, set one in front of Patricia and took his seat on the couch across from her. They both sipped from the glasses. Roland twirled the liquid in his glass, studying the ice cubes circling. He saw himself in that glass. Trapped like the ice cubes, only his barrier could not be seen or touched, but like the ice, Roland could not get out. The realization that this just might be the story of his career made it impossible to leave. Trapped by ambition, Roland Millhouse would ride this wave until he rode it out or drown.

"You have mentioned many times an evil within you. That is something I am having a problem wrapping myself around. I have never met a gentler, sweeter person. I have to say in my work I meet a lot of people. I interviewed a sicko who killed his wife and their two teenaged girls, then chopped them up and tossed the pieces into Lake Ontario. That is evil. How is there even a hint of evil in you?" he asked.

Patricia shrugged, opened the book, smoothed out the page as though it were cloth instead of paper. She did this every time, almost as though she were caressing the words.

Patricia's Journal—Wednesday, April 24, 1912

Mother didn't need to tell me not to go back to the McKinneys'. I don't think I can ever go back there.

But Dr. McKinney's house is not the only place to avoid in Kings Shore. I saw him tonight, Timmy Wilson. It was just after sunset, the sky in the west still had a tint of purple.

I was almost home when the boy jumped down from a tree. The oddest thing. He should have broken a leg, but he landed on his feet as steady as can be.

The moon was pale, but I could see that boy's eyes. They were as red as blood.

I shan't ever forget this night.

Daddy's home. Thanks be to God.

"What happened with the boy?" Roland asked.

"It was so horrible, I couldn't write it down. I was staring into those demon eyes, incapable of running. I couldn't even scream. I believed him to be dead. Can you imagine what it might be like to see a corpse standing before you?

Staring at you with eyes as red as blood."

She reached for her glass, and for the first time, Roland saw a tremor of age, or was it fear, as she raised it to her lips.

"He walked right up to me, still dressed in the little suit he had on when they closed the coffin, sealing him in. He held out his hand the way a child will do with an adult. It was like he wanted me to lead him to safety. My mind told me to run, but my hand reached out and took the boy's offered hand. Oh, it was so cold! Even on that warm night, his hand felt like ice. I tried to pull away then, but he was so strong. He squeezed my fingers until I cried out. Then he leaped up and wrapped his arms around my neck, and his legs around my waist, holding me like I was his momma. He rested his head on my shoulder. I held him to me. I didn't want to but it was an instinct, I think. To me, he was a child, until I felt the pain. It was terrible at first, then it went a bit numb."

She massaged the side of her neck with her right hand and wiped a single tear from her cheek with the left.

"Would you like to take a break?" Roland said.

"You're sweet," she said. She took another swallow of lemonade, and Roland did as well.

"Funny, the pain, it was so strong, I thought I might faint. But like I said, it didn't last, and the numb feeling that followed was pleasant. That boy had punctured my neck with teeth like no human ever had, and drew my blood into his mouth. I could hear him gulping. I didn't know then that it was my blood he was swallowing. I just remember it felt good, and whatever was causing that feeling, I didn't want to stop."

"Are you saying the boy was a vampire?"

"I guess that is what most would call him. Me, I called him evil."

"I saw all those headstones dated that spring. How is it you didn't die that night?" There was no judgment in his tone. No doubt. He wasn't all in yet, but he knew that whether the story was truth or fiction, it was true for Patricia.

"Daddy," she said. "He came home early. Word had reached him somehow about what was happening here, and he came as fast as he could. He happened home just when that Timmy thing was about to send me to the grave, or worse. I heard him holler, 'Demon, release my baby girl.'

"He did, too. Spun around and hissed at Daddy, just as Mrs. McKinney said. Daddy didn't falter though. Timmy was very strong, but he still weighed no more than a boy did. Daddy grabbed him by the hair and pulled him from me. It was awful the way he hissed and growled like an animal, all the while dangling from Daddy's outstretched hand. The tiny demon flailed its arms and legs at Daddy trying to get free. Like I said, it had great strength. When I saw Daddy's bruised arm, I almost cried.

"What came next caused me to faint straight away. The man who I knew to be as gentle as any human could be took his hunting knife and removed Timmy Wilson's head from his body. I can still hear my own scream as the cold black ick sprayed across my face. I gagged as some of that hideous demon's life force squirted into my open mouth. My head began to swoon from the gore and the loss of my own blood that Timmy had so tenderly pulled from my veins. The final blow came when that thing, dangling from Daddy's hand, no more body attached, looked at me. I don't mean it appeared to be looking. That little boy's red eyes saw me. It didn't die, not right away. It couldn't hiss anymore, but I think it was trying.

"That is all I remember from that night," she said. She took a long drink from her glass then sat looking at a painting of a couple who could only be her parents. Roland was sure she was looking at her father, and remembering the night he saved her from a monster.

Chapter 12

Roland sensed that his host had tired, and he excused himself. He drove into Kings Shore where he sat in a small café and ate a sandwich he barely remembered while feverishly stroking the keys of his laptop. Patricia's story was so fantastic that he didn't think recording it would be of any use. He was kicking himself now. This would not work as a fluff, human-interest yarn after the business report or right before the weather. This was going to be Roland's best seller.

After two hours of nonstop writing, Roland made his way to the library. It was a charming old two-story stone and brick building. He had no doubt that a young Miss Owens had been led through those doors by her mother a hundred plus years ago.

The library didn't have Wi-Fi, but the librarian did set him up with a network connection so he could get on the web. Roland banged away on the keyboard, entering one failed Google search after another. He found nothing on the internet to validate Patricia's tale. He understood a hundred years ago record keeping may have been lacking in an out-of-the-way town like Kings Shore, but he expected to find some mention of the events Patricia described. Not even the sights dedicated to urban legends had anything.

His next move was the basement. The librarian showed him to the microfiche room. He found nearly every small town and big city from Tobermory to Toronto had a paper at one time or another.

He was surprised to find that even Kings Shore had a newspaper back then. The paper closed fifty years ago. To his delight, the archives were converted to microfiche and stored in the library along with many of the rags from neighboring towns.

Roland spent the rest of the day, reading and searching for anything referring to Kings Shore, circa 1912. He was pleasantly surprised to find quite a lot. Nothing he found actually corroborated her story, but hints of it were there. Mysterious illnesses, sudden deaths, people attacked in the night.

At 8:00 p.m., a blue-haired old lady in a floral print dress and ortho-pedic shoes came down to usher him out.

"You've been down here so long we almost forgot you were here. If Lou Ann hadn't mentioned it, you might have gotten locked in," she said. "Did you find what you needed?"

"I may be back," he said. "Do you know any other place where I might be able to find local news from a hundred years ago?"

"Only one other place," she said. "George Stubing."

"Who is he?"

"He is a real historian. He studies for the pleasure of it. He lives about fifty miles south of town. Just follow the main road out of town for about a half hour. You'll see a roadside apple cider stand, turn right and drive until you see a long driveway lined with cedars. You can't miss it."

George Stubing's driveway couldn't be missed. The cedars were trimmed so perfectly, the drive looked like a country road in the Tuscan valley.

The entry to this house turned out to be false advertising at its best. With a grand entrance like this, one expected extravagant opulence, but the Stubing house was an ordinary middle-class ranch. The house had brick in the front and vinyl siding around the sides.

Roland guided his car between the immaculate trees. They ended in a teardrop drive in front of the house. A Canadian flag fluttered atop a white metal pole in the middle of the teardrop. Red and white impatiens surrounded the flagpole for an added touch of patriotic pride.

Roland was sure George was going to answer the door dressed in red and white, and singing "O Canada," or maybe the doorbell would play the anthem.

George answered the door after the first ring. "Yes?" he said as he looked at Roland standing on his porch. Blue jeans and a white threadbare t-shirt left Roland disappointed. His expectations were sorely missed when he took in George's attire.

"My name is Roland Millhouse, with CTV," Roland said, extending his right hand and hoping his disappointment didn't show. "Are you George Stubing?"

"Yes," George said, giving Roland's hand a brief shake.

"The lady at the library in Kings Shore suggested you might be able to help me," Roland said.

"Milly?" George asked.

"Actually, she didn't tell me her name. Nice lady, maybe sixty-five, flowers all over her dress," Roland said.

George smiled. "That's Milly, alright. What did Milly say I could help you with?"

"George, Milly speaks to your knowledge of history in very high regard," Roland said, hoping a compliment might make George more apt to cooperate. "I have been interviewing Patricia Owens for a story with the network, and I am hoping to get some background information on life in the Kings Shore area in 1912."

"What makes 1912 of interest to you?"

"Miss Owens took me to the cemetery, and there was a lot of death in the spring of that year."

George motioned Roland to the wicker chairs on the porch. The men sat, and George asked, "Did Patricia tell you about those graves?"

"She did," Roland said. "At least she has started. She was getting tired during our morning chat, so I left her to rest. I am a reporter, George. No matter who the source, I try to get facts to back up any claim."

"I can't fault you for that," George said.

"It keeps the lawyers at the station happy," Roland said.

"Of course I wasn't there like Patricia, and I haven't spoken with anyone who was. I have spoken to Patricia many times, but she has always been tightlipped about that time. I hope you will let me read her stories when you have them ready."

"I would be honored," Roland said. "Is there anything you can tell me about that spring?"

"I have heard tales of dark times," George said, his face crawing out to give him a distant look of sorrow. "The stories talk of demons, or monsters that stole women and children in the night. And, how just a few of these demons killed most of the men in town in a battle that was waged in a single night."

"You don't have any documents or news clippings from that time?" Roland asked.

"Sorry, son. I told you everything I can, aside from what I've read at the library. I'm sure you have exhausted your search there already, or you wouldn't be here."

Roland stood, stretched out his legs, extended his hand and said, "I thank you for your time."

"Don't mention it. If there is anything else I might be able to help you with, you know where I am."

"Indeed I do," Roland said, slipping into his car. "You really have a beautiful place here, George."

Before George could answer, Roland pulled the door closed and in seconds, was watching George disappear in his rearview mirror.

Chapter 13

"Good morning, young man," Patricia said when Roland got out of his car. "You look like a man on vacation. You should wear shorts more often; those are the whitest legs I have seen in some time."

Roland flushed a bit, and they both chuckled as he climbed the steps to meet her.

When he joined her in the shade of the veranda, concern filled his eyes. He looked down on her, seated in her favorite chair, like a queen on a throne. A very old-looking queen, he thought. Two days ago he couldn't believe this woman was over eighty; now he believed her all of her 120 years.

"Good morning, how are you today, Patricia?"

"Well, Roland, I am feeling a bit punk today. You know I haven't had an illness of any kind since the winter of 1911. I can't say I missed it."

"If that's true, then you are way overdue," he said with a grin. He tried to make light of her possible illness, but Roland knew that any illness in a woman her age could be deadly. His cavalier words were meant to put her at ease. Stressing over her health would not help her recover.

"I can't argue with that, Roland. I have to be honest though. This is most unpleasant."

"Maybe we should take the day off…"

"Roland," she interrupted. "I am too old to put things off. I need to tell my story while I'm still able."

"Okay, then," he said. "Tell me what happened the night your father returned."

"Like I told you yesterday, I have no memory of that night past the point where I fainted. The next thing I remember is waking in bed two days later. It was a trying time for Mother. Mother and Daddy both thought I'd been infected with the sickness. She was sure I was going to die like the others. Daddy, not being here when the others passed, just worried that the traumatic events I had witnessed might harm me mentally."

"I can't imagine a parent who wouldn't worry about that," Roland said.

Patricia pulled the front of her sweater tight around her neck. The morning sun had chased the night chill from the air two hours ago. Roland sat in shorts and a t-shirt, with the first hint of sweat beading at his brow, and she was fighting off a chill.

"Mother was sleeping in a chair next to my bed when I woke. I was so hungry," Patricia said through a chuckle. "I was very young, and I hadn't eaten in over two days. Of course, I didn't know how long it had been. I only knew that I was starving. So, I nudged Mother awake and asked her if breakfast was ready."

Patricia laughed again, and Roland joined her.

"Mother threw her arms around my neck and squeezed me so tight I thought I would faint dead away all over again. Then she ran from the room calling for Daddy. I thought she was being silly, so I got up, feeling better than I ever had, in spite of my hunger. Can you picture it? I hadn't had the slightest morsel, nor had I anything to drink, in over two days. I should have been wobbly legged and miserable."

"I know I would be," Roland said.

"Well, I put on my robe and went to the kitchen."

"Was your mother in the kitchen?"

"No, but Annie was. Annie was our maid. She hugged me tighter than Mother. She was very strong for a tiny thing. I thought I might break."

"Was your maid always so friendly?" Roland asked with raised brows.

"Annie was a dear woman," Patricia said. Her eyes looked out toward the road as if she were trying to see the lake through the trees. The sun shone bright, causing her to squint. She strained to see something in the far-off shadows of the garden shrubbery. "She was always nice to me from the time I was a girl. When I awoke, she was filled with joy for a child she loved like her own."

"Did she know what happened to you? With Timmy Wilson, I mean."

"No. She was told I had fallen ill. All, including Annie, were sure it was the same affliction that took the Wilsons.

"Mrs. Wilson?" Roland asked. "The last you mentioned she was recovering at the McKinneys'."

"While I was in bed, Mrs. Wilson succumbed to the illness. Dr. McKinney said she screamed out in the early evening of the night I was attacked. The night Daddy returned. Mrs. McKinney ran directly to her, but she was already gone. They told Daddy that she had a look of terror on her face. Her expression did not relax in death. The poor woman went to her grave with that expression."

"Weren't you attacked in the early evening?" Roland asked.

"Very good," she said, patting his hand with hers. "You may be catching on. It is believed that poor Mrs. Wilson succumbed the moment Daddy slew the monster that once was Timmy Wilson. No one could know for sure. Daddy didn't look at his watch the moment he took the life from Timmy. If it even was life. The McKinneys couldn't give an exact time of death for Mrs. Wilson either. All we know is they both happened just after sunset.

"Before Annie could prepare a meal for me, Daddy came charging into the kitchen, followed by Mother. I ran to him and hugged him the way Annie had hugged me. I kissed him on his cheeks, over and over. I think some of it was gratitude for saving me, but most was just being happy to see him.

"He instructed Annie to feed me, and told me to join him in his study when I had eaten and got myself dressed proper."

Patricia's Journal—April 28, 1912
    I slept for 2 days.

Daddy is home. He arrived just in time to save me from Timmy Wilson. The poor boy had become a monster. He was drinking the blood right from my neck.

Dear God.

Daddy beheaded the thing. That image will haunt me all my days.

Daddy told me this morning that he burned the remains of Timmy Wilson. He said the thing's eyes continued to look around 10 minutes after he cut the head from the boy's body.

May God watch over us all.

"Can you imagine?" Patricia asked Roland. "The terror Daddy felt that night. First to get home just as a boy he knew had latched onto my throat and drew the very blood from my veins. Then to see that same child squeal and growl like a wild dog. To see that innocent-looking face peering around, trying to speak after being removed from its body must surely have been unimaginable."

She wiped a tear from her cheek and reached for a tissue in the pocket of her sweater.

"Shall I get us something to drink?" he asked.

"I think maybe it's time to go inside anyway. If you don't mind, there is a tray on the counter in the kitchen. Bring it to the sitting room, would you?"

"Of course," he said and stood. He held out a hand, and for the first time, Patricia accepted his help.

Chapter 14

Roland entered the sitting room to a familiar scene: Patricia seated on the couch with her journal placed on her lap. Her hands rested neatly on the book, folded like those of a schoolgirl awaiting her teacher's instructions. She didn't acknowledge his presence when he entered. She just stared out the window. Her gaze focused, yet nothing in her line of sight was remarkable in even the vaguest sense. Roland didn't think the beautiful weather held her attention. He doubted she was looking at anything, or seeing anything for that matter. If he had to guess, he would have said that whatever Patricia focused on could be seen only in her memories of 1912.

Roland set the tray on the coffee table. Without asking, he poured her a glass of lemonade and then one for himself. The glass clunked slightly as he placed it on the side table next to her. That seemed to bring Patricia back to the present. She smiled up at him and he returned it with a grin he hoped did not show the concern he felt. After she sampled from the glass, Roland took his seat in the chair across from his host. He chugged down half his drink, grimaced with pleasure at the sweet-sour icy beverage.

As if she were reacting to instructions from backstage, Patricia opened the journal and caressed the page with the usual brush of her hand.

How wonderful and dreadful, he thought. To hold such emotion and longing for the memories, both good and bad, contained in the pages of her book.

Patricia's Journal—Monday, June 10, 1912
   All has been quiet since Daddy returned. No one has spoke of Timmy, and we buried Mrs. Wilson. I am so saddened when I walk by the Wilson place. The whole family taken by the sickness.
   That's what they are calling it. The Sickness.
   Things are getting back to normal since no new sicknesses have occurred in almost 2 weeks.
   Maybe God is watching over us.

Patricia's Journal—Tuesday, June 11, 1912
   As if to mock my words of yesterday, the bodies of three strangers were found in the woods near the mill. I heard the constable tell Daddy that they all looked like the boy when he was found.
   I assume he means Timmy.

"That was the day things really turned ugly in Kings Shore," Patricia said. She was looking directly into Roland's eyes, as though she were trying to assess how he grasped her meaning.

"The sickness was accelerating?" Roland asked.

"There was no sickness, Roland. I think by now you have figured that out. That was just what we were calling it because we didn't know what else to call it."

He nodded, and they both took a sip of lemonade. Roland took comfort from those sips. It was something he could feel and taste and smell. It was real, and if this was reality, he could convince himself that Patricia's tale was just the ramblings of an old woman. Deep down, he didn't believe that, but it helped to keep him in his seat when what he really wanted was to run.

"Those men had no identification. Nobody in town recognized any of them. These were strangers in the truest sense of the word. They are buried in unmarked graves in the woods where they were found. It seems unchristian to dig a hole and pitch the bodies of three men in. To cover them without so much as a prayer, but that's what was done. Not even a pine box. They just tossed all three in one hole and filled it in. Some justified it by saying the illness was brought here by them, and bringing their remains into town might just infect more people."

"They were scared," Roland said. "You can't blame them for trying to take care of their own."

"You have a keen ear, Roland. That is exactly what they were. They wanted to believe it was those men, what brought this plague on us. That way they could convince themselves that with them being buried out in the woods, all our problems were buried with them."

"But things got worse. Didn't they?"

Patricia nodded, and she began to stroke the journal. The swish of her delicate hands on the paper made the hair stand up on Roland's arms and neck.

Swish, swish, swish. Her delicate fingers slid over the paper almost as though she were trying to banish the evil from the pages.

Patricia's Journal—Wednesday, June 12, 1912

The church bell rang just before 10:00. Daddy rushed into town with Bill, the stableman. I wish he'd stayed home. I know it is more of the sickness. I just know.

I sat in the parlor with Mother, waiting.

Not knowing is torture. If only we could leave this hell.

"It was the men from the woods wasn't it?" Roland asked.

"When Daddy got to the church, most of the men from town were there. A few arrived just after. The strangers they buried in the woods walked into town. Four of the men Daddy met in town that day were present when those three men were buried. All four were at the church. And do you know what, Roland?"

"None of those four protested the claim that three men they knew to be dead and buried walked into town," Roland said.

"Bingo," Patricia said, reaching across the coffee table and slapping him on the knee.

It was a gesture of recognition, but Roland took no glee in the praise he received. Roland's gaze had drifted to the same window he earlier witnessed Patricia staring through. The scenery had grown no more remarkable over the short time since she had fixed on it. Roland needed a moment, and the summer sky invited him in.

Chapter 15

"Daddy didn't return home until well past midnight. Mother and I went to bed around 10:00 p.m. like we always did, but I couldn't sleep, and I don't think Mother got a wink either. Not until Daddy was home safe."

"Did he say what happened?"

"Not that night," Patricia said. "We, Mother and I, didn't let on that we were still awake. Daddy walked past my closed door, and it took all the willpower I could muster not to run out and throw my arms around him. I suspected that whatever he had been through that night weighed on him something awful, so I stayed in bed. And I heard not a peep from him when he closed their bedroom door behind him, so I knew that Mother was feigning sleep also."

The room had gone suddenly dark. Roland and Patricia looked to the window. The odds of the clouds moving to block out the sun, just as Patricia's tale and mood turned morose, seemed more than coincidence to Roland. He walked over to the window to investigate the source of the gloom.

"Looks like rain," he said.

She didn't rise to check herself. She didn't even bother to look out the window from her seat.

"It'll blow over before you know it."

"You're a meteorologist, too?" he teased.

"Sonny, when you have seen as many days as I have, you get a feel for what mother nature is going to send your way. Those clouds out there are just hanging around to give us a little mood lighting."

Roland shrugged, pulled the curtain back where it was and returned to his seat. "Did your father talk about it the next day?"

"Daddy didn't, he kept things tight to the vest if you know what I mean. Bill, the stableman, on the other hand, was a bit of a gossip," she said with a giggle.

"You went and pumped him for information?"

"I sure as hell didn't need to prime that pump. Once that man got talking, there was no stopping him. He told me about the men, meeting at the church. That the three strangers were seen in town. They hunted those men all night. Not even Wilf Durham's bloodhounds could get a trail on them. So do you know what those men did?"

"They dug up the grave in the woods," Roland said without a moment's hesitation. "To prove to themselves that it wasn't the same men."

Patricia gave an exaggerated nod. "Exactly. They all thought the graves had looked disturbed, but it was in the woods. It's hard to say what kind of animal might have pawed around in the fresh-dug ground.'

"You're going to tell me it was empty, aren't you? The grave I mean."

She nodded her head the same way. "Of course, it was a lot easier to dig up, being a fresh grave, so it didn't take them any time at all. Do you know what the odd thing was about that grave? Aside from the corpses being missing, that is."

Roland shrugged. He was getting a feel for this tale, but he couldn't think of anything that could be considered odd. Digging up a fresh grave to find it empty had to be near the top of the oddity scale. What could they possibly have found to rival that?

"Everything in that hole that should have been alive was dead. The bugs, worms, and ants littered the soil like tiny little corpses. The things that should have been dead were strolling around like they were going to the town meeting, while every manner of crawling thing in that hole was stone cold dead. A great shiver ran down Bill's spine when he told me that. I thought he was shining me on until I saw the way he shivered. Bill was scared, and frightened people don't try to shine you on."

"You believed his story?" he said.

"Not at first. My whole life, Bill had been around. He was so full of stories that the other hands would respond with 'Sure Bill,' whenever they thought someone was spinning a yarn. So, at first, I thought he might just be making light of a dark scene. I could tell early on that he was telling the truth this time. That poor man had terror in his eyes. You can't fake that kind of fear."

"Patricia," Roland said, "I know that people are not inclined to leave their every possession, but it seems to me that when things begin to go south that fast, it's time to get out of Dodge."

"What you have to keep in mind young man, is this all took place a hundred years ago. There was but one road out of town, and it wasn't much of a road. It cut right through some heavily forested land. For fifty miles, towering trees lined the road on both sides."

"But if they left first thing in the morning," he reasoned.

"There weren't many cars in Kings Shore in 1912. Two, maybe three if you count the truck thing they had at the mill. Everyone else was still traveling by horse and wagon. Fifty miles was a two-day journey at best. Not to the next town, mind you. That would only get you by the forest and into some open ground."

"Which means they would have had to spend the night out there," he said.

"Exposed to them."

Patricia nodded, adding, "We didn't know until much later that those demons only came out at night. So in the beginning, the people were just as frightened about traveling in the daylight."

"When did you find out about their aversion to sunlight?"

That brought a grin to the old woman's face, removing some of the years that seemed to have grown there over the past few days. She flipped open her journal, smoothed out the pages, and took a drink of lemonade.

Roland emptied his glass, refilled it, sipped again, and waited for her to read from the book.

Patricia's Journal—Monday, June 17, 1912

The men from town caught one of the strangers. One of the men they had buried in the woods. There was no celebration with the man's apprehension. While this one was secured, the other two got hold of Bill and dragged him off before he could be rescued.

They thought to bring the stranger to the jail. The search for Bill begins in the daylight.

It was dawn when they led the stranger across the common to the jail.

They say that as soon as the sun's rays touched the stranger's skin, he screamed like an animal. His face and hands blistered, and his skin started to smoke. The demon man fell to the ground, writhing and screaming.

They told me he burst into flames right there on the ground.

When he finished burning, nothing remained but a stain on the ground. No ash, no bones, just blackened earth.

Chapter 16

Patricia had grown tired, leaving Roland to fend for himself. He didn't feel right rummaging through her fridge, so he got in his car and headed for town. While he drove, he rewound the tape in his recorder and pushed Play.

Patricia's strained voice filled the silence with ominous dread. He had already heard her tell this part, but hearing it again enclosed in the car, her words had nowhere to go but into his brain. Whatever doubt Roland was hanging onto for the sake of his peace of mind slipped away.

At dawn, every able-bodied man in town went into the woods searching for Bill. They started at the place where the two demon men dragged him off. More than fifty men and a dozen boys who were no more than fifteen went into the woods to find Bill.

They fanned out, working their way into the forest. It was painstakingly slow. At noon, they took their lunch on the shore of Cornatha Creek. They found one of Bill's boots in the beginning of the search, but that was all.

After lunch, the search party proceeded east in single file, then made their way back to the start. By then some women folk had brought dinner. Some ate on wagons, others just sat on the ground. Not like today where people tote lawn chairs everywhere they go.

There was only time left for a quick circumference search adjacent to the starting point, and then everybody rushed home. Funny seeing so many grown people rush home as though they were afraid of the dark. Of course, it wasn't the dark that scared them. It was what lurked in the shadows of those trees. By now, everyone had dropped the pretense of an illness.

Demons were living in Kings Shore as sure as the sun would drop below the horizon after dusk. In another month, we would normally be looking forward to the sunset, to get relief from the heat of the day. Nobody had air conditioning, remember. That spring we would have welcomed hot, humid days without any sunset.

It was just before ten when a knock came on the door. Daddy was home, but he was exhausted from the search, so I went to answer the door. He yelled for me to stop. I was so frightened I almost made water in my knickers. Daddy had never yelled at me, not ever.

I looked to him wide-eyed and frightened. My heart was pounding in my chest, and my head went a bit fuzzy. Daddy ran at me. I backed away, but when he got close, I didn't see anger in his eyes. It was fear. I had never seen fear on that man's face until that night.

He looked through the sidelight, then told me to fetch his scattergun. It was a heavy old thing. I was a grown woman, and I could barely lift it. Daddy took it in one hand, pulled back the hammer and called through the door.

"Who's there?" he said.

Nobody answered. We heard some odd scratching, like a cat or maybe a raccoon trying to get in.

"I'm armed," Daddy called through the door.

Scritch, scritch, scritch, on the wooden door. All the doors were made of heavy wood. Not like the steel things they put on houses now. Daddy pushed his face against the sidelight trying to see who was on the other side.

Just when he began to tell me there was nobody there, I saw him through the window. It was Bill. At least it was what used to be Bill. All the humor was gone from his face. He stood by the window, staring at me. When Daddy came to see what I was looking at, Bill disappeared.

I told him Bill was out there. I thought Daddy would rush outside to welcome his old friend back, but he just pushed the curtain aside and, crouching, he looked out into the dark. He looked left and right and down. No Bill.

I screamed again, and when Daddy saw what I was screaming at, he fell on his backside. Bill's face was looking down on us from the top of the window. He was upside down. His eyes were black holes, like his eyeballs had been replaced by big black pearls. Seeing him hanging like that made me remember the story Mrs. McKinney told me about Timmy Wilson crawling around the side of the house like a spider.

Daddy raised the gun, pointing it right at Bill's head.

"Daddy," I said. "It's Bill."

"No, darling girl," he said. "That thing just looks like Bill."

Daddy pulled the trigger, and Bill's head exploded. Oh, how my ears hurt when that gun fired. My hands sprang up to suppress the sound, but of course, it was much too late for that.

I saw Bill's body drop. It fell like a stone to the garden below the window. I stood there, hands over my ears, screaming. Screaming and crying. I didn't know until that moment how much I loved that silly old man. Bill was like the uncle I never had.

Daddy hollered at me to go to my room. I refused.

He said, "Fine, girl. If you're going to be around, then you will have to help. The first thing you need to do is stop crying. There will be plenty of time for that later for both of us." I don't mind saying, that stopped my crying right then and there. I had never considered ever seeing Daddy cry.

I could never have imagined what he meant by help. I followed him outside, and he went right to Bill's body. I was horrified and wanted to look away. But I could no more look away than I could stop breathing. I used to sit on that man's knee and listen to him tell stories. Now he lay in what remained of the spring tulips, minus his head anyway.

Daddy handed me the gun and the lantern that I hadn't even noticed him carrying, then he took hold of Bill's ankles and dragged him across the lawn. Daddy was a big strong man, but by the time he got around be-hind the barn, he was exhausted. He dropped Bill's feet to the ground, and rested with his hands on his knees, gasping for breath.

I never would have believed Daddy capable of what came next. He took the lantern from my hand and tossed it down on the body. Nothing happened at first. It didn't break, so the grotesque sight was illuminated in a macabre eeriness.

Daddy raised the gun again and said, "Lord forgive me," and fired one round at the lantern. The lamp oil sprayed all over, and Bill turned into a hideous bonfire spewing acrid black smoke.

Roland paused the player. He stopped at the intersection of Maple and Divine and stared at the flashing red light on the recorder.

"Jesus, Patricia," Roland said to the empty car. "How the hell did you ever live with this all these years and stay sane?" He pushed Play to re-sume listening.

You can't imagine the heat. The flame in the lamp was a bright shade of yellow and orange. The searing heat coming from Bill's corpse glowed white. The black smoke spewing up from those white flames was preter-natural.

The fire roared like a blow torch until it nearly burned out. Once the flames and smoke cleared away, all that remained was a scorched stain on the ground.

The story Bill told me about the stranger catching fire and the mark left on the ground afterward made me miss the old man right then. I looked down at the blackened earth, and I swear I heard his voice say-ing, "There was nothing left but a black stain on the ground.'

Daddy saw the tears on my cheek and said, "It's as good a time to cry as there ever was."

I looked up to see tears in Daddy's eyes. Not before, and not after did I ever see tears in Daddy's eyes.

Chapter 17

Roland spent the rest of the afternoon and early evening going over the previous tapes. He sat at the small desk in his room at the B&B, his laptop open and his voice recorder ready. He would listen to a passage, pause, type notes into his computer, then continue. He tried his best to fill in the blanks from the sessions he forgot to record.

He emailed the copy and photos of the fluff piece on Patricia's 120th birthday and requested a two-week vacation. He didn't anticipate any problem with the request since the network still owed him three weeks carryover from the previous year.

He would spend the two weeks with Patricia. He would get her story, and write a novel. He could never sell it as a memoir. As nonfiction, it could only find a home in the rags that print stories of alien autopsies, and women who claim to have had sex with Bigfoot.

He would change the names and places to protect the innocent, or guilty. To maintain copyright, of course, and ensure that he didn't have to share the proceeds with the Patricia Owens estate. He didn't want to be crass, but she was 120, and at the rate of her decline in the few days since meeting her, he had his doubts that she would live to see the book in print.

Roland returned to the old house just after 7:30 p.m. Patricia was sitting on the porch. On the table beside her sat a pitcher and two glasses.

Roland gave her a wave, and she returned it with a smile, the smile from a few days earlier. The rest had miraculously restored her to a degree. She hadn't captured the vibrancy of the day Roland first met her, but she had the look of a much younger woman than the person he left earlier in the day. Her smile betrayed the improved appearance, however. Roland saw through her bravado somehow. He saw a smile, not of happiness but of deceit. Patricia was trying to convince him that all was well, but her eyes conveyed the truth and Roland began to worry more than ever that she was ill, and with a woman her age every illness is life-threatening.

Roland cared for this old woman. He liked her as a person and respected her bravery more than he had anyone.

"Did you rest well?" he asked her.

"I did," she said, her smile widening a bit.

"I sent off your birthday story to the network along with some pictures. I hope you don't mind."

"That is why you came, isn't it?"

"It was," he said. "I came to get the birthday story, I stayed to get your story."

"Of course, dear boy, do sit," she said, motioning to the other chair. "Pour yourself a glass of tea."

Roland filled his glass, topped up Patricia's and settled in beside her.

"You say you are staying?" she asked.

"I asked for two weeks off."

"Did you," she said. It could have been a question, but Roland understood it for the statement it was meant to be. What he heard in her words was, "I knew you would not leave without the whole story."

"Do you think you can put up with me for a while longer?" he asked.

"I have to admit," she said. "I am surprised. I thought after today's talk you would have left thinking I was either crazy, senile or fiendish."

"Or all of the above," he said with a wink and a grin.

She shrugged, sipped her tea but said nothing.

Roland looked down at the tray with the pitcher and two glasses on it. "Are you expecting another guest or was it that obvious that I would be back?"

"Well," she said with a grin. "I had some doubts you would return, but I was very much hoping you would. Truth be told, my doubts were quite small."

The sun sitting low in the sky cast long shadows. Patricia stood, picked up her journal and said, "Let's go around back for a bit." It was the first time he had been in the back of the house. The entire backyard was shaded by the big house at this time of day. The leaves on the big sycamore hung limp in the still air. It was a warm evening; Roland wore a short-sleeved polo and cargo shorts. Patricia had her typical flowery dress, but tonight she had also put on a grey cable-knit cardigan.

The sweater in this heat was one more thing to convince Roland that Patricia wasn't doing as well as she claimed. The porch behind the house sported the same furnishings as the front. Wicker chairs, divided by a matching table. He set the tray down and helped her into her seat.

The backyard looked much the same as the front. It was cared for in a way that told visitors, "We do what we can. No more, no less." A hundred yards or so from the back porch, an old barn still holding true angles looked an odd monolith in a sea of pines and spruces framing the back of the property.

Looking at the barn, Roland said, "Patricia, what happened after Bill's body was incinerated?"

"When we got back to the house," she said, "Mother was standing on the porch." Roland saw Patricia looking off into the distance.

He had seen Patricia do this many times, and he knew now that some parts of her story were just that, a story. Stories relayed and retold, if only to the shadows and maybe Scuba. Something that happened so long ago it ceased to be memory and became lore.

There were times like this when telling it caused her to relive the memory inside her mind. When Patricia Owens went back to spring 1912, she needed a moment to regroup before coming back to the now. Assembling the next chapter of her tale in her mind had sent her back, and Roland sat in silence waiting for her return.

She looked slightly confused when she came back to him, and Roland waited patiently until she was ready to continue. She looked into his eyes, smiled awkwardly, then sipped her tea. Roland recognized the sips as another of her stall tactics. When she needed a moment, she either went off somewhere inside herself, or sipped her beverage, or caressed her journal.

"Mother wanted to know what we were up to," Patricia continued, her voice barely audible. "Daddy told her that one of the horses foundered and had to be put down. He told her we burned the remains behind the barn so the animals didn't come around."

"Quick thinking," Roland said. "How did he explain the gunshot in the house and the broken window?"

"Bravo, young man," she said. "Daddy told her he dropped his rifle tripping over her damn cat." She laughed out loud at that. "Daddy hated Mother's cat and took not just a small amount of joy in blaming the poor thing. That cat wasn't even in the house when the window got shot out."

"Your father was very fast on his feet, wasn't he?"

"Daddy never lost an argument," she said. "He was the smartest man I ever met. And I have lived a long time, so that's saying something. I must say though, Roland. Your insight is making me think you might have been able to give Daddy a run for his money."

"Thank you, Patricia. I'm honored to be considered as potential for inclusion in that esteemed company."

"You're too polite," she said, patting his knee.

"Mother believed Daddy's excuses. At least she claimed to. I think she may have wanted to believe them because the alternative, based on events of the time, was much more grim."

Roland nodded and sipped from his glass. Scuba ambled over and, without warning, leaped onto Roland's lap causing him to make a squeaky sort of yip. The cat didn't seem to notice, or didn't care. He just turned himself away from Roland, stretched out and fell asleep on Roland's warm thighs.

"Would you like to know the truth?" Roland asked, looking at Patricia, his mouth drawn into a forced smile. "I don't really like cats."

"I think he knows," she said. "I can't tell you how many times I have seen a cat cozy up to people who apparently were not fond of cats. It seems the more someone dislikes the animals, the more they want to prove the humans wrong. Almost as if the cats are thinking, 'If I am nice to him, he will like me.' Do you know what I mean?"

"I thought you said cats didn't really care what we thought."

"I believe that to be true, but everyone wants to be liked. Even cats. Once he wins you over, he will ignore you forever."

Without even thinking about it, Roland began to stroke Scuba's head and scratch behind his ears. The cat stretched out further on his lap, purred loud enough to be heard inside the house, and gingerly nuzzled his head against Roland's belly.

"I think Scuba's work might just be done here," Patricia said motioning to Roland's fingers caressing his furry friend.

"You might be right," he said.

With that, Scuba jumped off and trotted around to the front of the house.

chapter 18

After a light meal of sandwiches and fruit, Roland and Patricia resumed their seats on the front porch. The breeze that had cooled the afternoon had blown itself out making the air feel warmer. Patricia removed her sweater and draped it over the porch railing. In the fading light of what was a stunning sunset, she opened her journal.

"Daddy had no quick excuse for this. He just asked me to take Mother back inside. I tried to take her arm and lead her away, but she clung to Daddy so tight it was no use. He took her inside himself. I went to the barn and started filling buckets from the hand pump. I toted ten pails of water to that spot. Poured it over the black *ick*, and it still looked grotesque."

Patricia pointed to the left side of the house. "See that sickly rose bush?"

Roland nodded, but she was looking at the bush and could not have seen him.

"The land is sick where that bush is. Anything that touches the evil from within those dreadful creatures turns ugly.

"That day, Daddy hitched a pair of horses and drew a wagon over to that spot. Well, almost to that spot. When those horses got to within a couple of yards from there, they reared and bucked and refused to go any further. Daddy unhitched them, and the two of us pushed that wagon the rest of the way. We took shovels and dug up that dirt. We dug until any sign of the black gore and the water I dumped there had been removed. That left us with a problem. Can you guess what our problem was?"

"With the wagon filled with dirt, it was too heavy to move by hand," he answered.

"Give the man a prize," she cheered. "Daddy would have liked you a great deal, Roland."

"So how did you get the wagon out of there?"

"The motor car," she said. "That pathetic little thing struggled, but once the wagon started to move it was okay. We towed the wagon to the edge of the cliff down by the lake and pushed it off. Daddy said that the horses would never come near it again anyway."

"That must have been a sight to see."

"I have to admit, in a time before moving pictures and television, watching a wagon smash to bits on the rocks was something."

"How did you fill in the hole?"

"The same way we made it," she said. "Daddy hitched a different pair of horses to another wagon. We filled it with dirt from the new pasture. Daddy wanted to dig a pond in that pasture anyway, so that day we got it started."

"Did the horses pull the wagon all the way up?"

"They did. Daddy stuffed their noses with something so they wouldn't smell anything if there was anything left to smell. Those animals were skittish as hell, but they managed to do their job."

Roland looked at the solitary rose bush in the garden beside the porch. The thorns were abnormally long, and he could swear some had barbs on them like fishhooks. The branches were thick at the base with a coarse bark that left it doubtful that it was a rose bush at all. The leaves definitely looked like rose leaves in shape, but the color was too green, and the veins in the leaves had a red tinge to them.

"What color are the flowers?" he asked.

"That bush has been there for ninety-nine years. I planted it myself because none of the annuals that Mother once planted would grow there. I would plant them on Monday, and by Tuesday they would be withered. I had this rose bush shipped from Europe. It has managed to stay alive but has never produced a single rose. That ground is damned with the blood of demons," she whispered.

Chapter 19

Patricia stood. "Young man, what say we walk awhile. These old bones don't forgive too much sitting. It's as fine an evening for a walk as ever there was."

Obediently, Roland stood and strode to the steps, where he waited for his host. She took his arm with her left hand while her right held the banister.

"I think I might have to find a smaller place to live soon," she said. They both knew that would not happen. She was born in this house. Aside from a short stay in town in the spring of 1912, she had lived her whole life in this house. It was unthinkable that Patricia Owens would live anywhere but this house.

"Well, Patricia, I can say without hesitation that you are the only person in Canada who has had the same address for 120 years."

That brought a smile to her face as they made their way past Roland's car.

"On second thought, Roland," she said. "Would you care to take me for a ride in that pretty car of yours?"

Without saying a word, he took his keys out, pressed a button on the fob to unlock the doors, and opened the passenger side door.

"I left my journal on the porch," she announced.

Roland closed the door and trotted back to the house. When he returned to the car, he had her journal under his arm and their glasses in his hands.

After stowing the glasses in the cup holders and placing the book in her lap, he guided the car to the road. She pointed to her left, and they were off.

"What did you do after you filled in the hole in front of the house?" he asked.

"The clouds moved in as we were finishing. The sky turned angry in a hurry as though it weren't happy with our activity. Or, maybe mother earth hoped to lend a hand by sending some rain to wash away anything we may have missed."

They both looked to the sky to make sure a repeat performance wasn't rolling in to protest the telling of this secret. The quarter moon illuminated some fluffy clouds high in the atmosphere. The sky would not drop any moisture tonight.

"We retired to the house after that," she continued. "I was reading something, but I can't for the life of me remember what."

Roland was sure he could give her a pass on that. The fact that she could remember her own name at her age was a miracle. The last book he read had some self-help theme and an odd title he couldn't remember, and that was only two weeks ago.

"Daddy went to bed. I knew things were going to the devil when my father went to bed before dark."

"He had been under a great deal of stress, and was sleep deprived; his actions seem reasonable to me," Roland said.

"For most that would be true, dear," she replied. "Daddy, you have to understand, was not most people. He slept into the next day. When he woke, he found Mother knitting in her chair beside the bed. I don't know how he slept with those needles clicking relentlessly. Maybe it gave him peace to know she was there. Anyway, he slept until the church bells rang just after sunset. Can you imagine sleeping for more than a full day?"

"I remember doing it once," Roland said. "Between work and finals at the U, I was awake for thirty-eight straight hours. When I finally slept,

I was out for eighteen hours. When I woke up, I felt exhausted."

She nodded like she understood and said, "I bet Daddy felt the same, but when the bells chimed, he didn't have time to be tired.

"I heard those bells, and a second later I heard his heavy footsteps on the floor over my head. He came running down the stairs, pulling his suspenders over his shoulders as he did. Mother followed along in his wake trying to convince him that the men in town could handle this crisis without him.

"I too pleaded with him not to go. Of course, he did anyway," Patricia said as she opened the journal.

Patricia's Journal—Thursday, June 20, 1912
    Daddy has gone to town. It was those bells again.
    Please, God, watch over him.
    Mother has gone to her room. We are both sick with worry.

"He did, you know," Patricia said. "That night at least. God watched over us all that night. When Daddy got to the common, the men were gathered at the bandstand. It was a wonderful place before this all happened. During the summer, the town would gather in the common, sometimes bands would play. People would dance and sing. It was a glorious, innocent time. The innocence died when Timmy disappeared, and it never came back. Not ever.

"No band played that night. Just angry frightened farmers and loggers." She paused like she was looking for a memory in the back of her mind.

"Patricia," Roland said. "With Bill gone, who told you about this night?"

"Daddy," she said. "He sat Mother and me down the next day and told us everything. Of course, I already knew a great deal, but it was all new to Mother, and she didn't take it well.

"When Daddy arrived in the common he learned that two more men had gone missing. If it was a couple of single men, you could say they decided to cut and run before they became victims, but these were family men with wives and children and property.

"Daddy asked where their families were. The men said they were at home behind locked doors. They seemed quite pleased to tell Daddy that news. Daddy split the group in half, and one went to check on the new widows. Of course, there was no evidence that they were widows, but no one was under the impression that the end for those men would be any different than it had been for the others.

"Daddy's group went to the Mitchell place. The trip out there was uneventful. When they got to the farm, however, the two strangers who had taken Bill into the woods were walking away from the front door. Daddy called for them to stop. They just hissed and descended the porch steps. Daddy said the hiss was the same one that boy gave before Daddy cut his head off."

She stopped and sipped her drink. Condensation dripped from the glass. Patricia wiped a drop of tea from her lower lip and set the glass back in the cupholder.

"Did the strangers surrender?" Roland asked.

"No, they just ambled toward the road like they were on a Sunday stroll. John Harris raised his gun, and when those demons heard him cock it, they sprang. That is the only way to describe what happened next. One second they were there, the next they weren't."

Roland had trouble envisioning this. "You mean they vanished? Like magic?"

"No magic involved. Just inhuman strength. They jumped into the air so high and so fast the posse saw neither where they went or how they got there. When they landed, it was cat-like. They dropped into position right behind Daddy's group. Before any of Daddy's men could react, four men were down. The remaining four spun and opened fire. Both of those strangers took two rounds in the chest. The force did knock them back, but it didn't knock them off their feet, and it certainly didn't kill them. Daddy said the shirts glistened with blackness as unspeakable foulness erupted from the wounds. It must have hurt them because they fled without any further confrontation. Daddy's men emptied their guns in the direction those things went, but it was doubtful any more damage was done."

At a stop sign, Roland ejected a tape from his recorder and inserted another. He slid the used tape into his shirt pocket, and asked, "What about the men? The four you said were down?"

"Dead, all of them. They fell to the ground face first. When they were turned over to check on their condition, one of them had a broken neck. His head flopped around without resistance. Every muscle, tendon, and bone had been twisted beyond what was possible. Another one had a hole in his chest. His heart sat on the ground beside him, lifeless, shining with blood, in the moonlight. The creature plunged his hand through the fellow's chest, grabbed his still-beating heart and yanked it out."

"I've seen that in movies," Roland said.

"Art mimics reality."

"Macabre art," he added.

Patricia shrugged. "Two of the men on the ground left a family behind. Philip Green had two little girls and a pregnant wife. We buried those two the next day. At least they stayed buried. Their wives and children moved into town. It wasn't safe for anyone on a secluded farm, and certainly not for women and children."

They traveled in silence for a bit, Patricia giving an occasional instructtion, and about ten minutes later he stopped the car at the edge of an escarpment overlooking the lake.

Chapter 20

Roland marveled at the view. Steps from the front of his car, the ground disappeared. He put the windows down at Patricia's request. The rhythmic swish of the waves rolling in on the sand twenty feet below played like the soporific melody of a sleep aid.

The moonlight danced on the surface of the lake. Lines of light reached out from a passing freighter as if casting a lifeline to shore. Everything for as far as the eye could see was black. Everything that is, but the moon, the stars and the light from the ship.

"It's beautiful," Roland said.

"Yes, it is. Ever since I was old enough to leave home alone, this has been my favorite place on earth. I am not alone in that. It has been the place for amorous youngsters to go to escape prying eyes. You know what I mean, Roland?"

"This is the make-out place for the local teens?" he asked.

"I guess that would be an accurate assessment. It has had that distinction since before I ever came here. The summer of 1912 didn't change that."

"I have done a couple of stories involving teens. As long as there have been people, teens have refused to listen to their parents when it came to advice on staying safe. The teens of 1912 didn't listen either, did they?"

Patricia opened the car door and eased herself from her seat. Roland did as well, quick-stepping to her side. He stumbled twice on the uneven ground before getting to her and had great concern for her footing.

"You're right," she said. "A group of kids snuck out of the house. A boy named Jimmy Alberts brought three bottles of his father's homemade wine. They made a big fire. There were seven of them. They found one of them down there." Patricia pointed to the rocks directly below where she stood. "Nobody knows what happened. The rest were never seen again."

Patricia paused, staring down to the water's edge. The white rocks glowed in the moonlight.

"Never seen alive again," she said and wiped a tear from her cheek with the back of her hand.

"They were seen in town again though, weren't they?" Roland asked.

She nodded, "Right in the town common. All six of them. They frolicked around on the bandstand and rolled around on the grass like normal teenagers.

"Auntie watched the whole thing from her upstairs window. They looked like they were having so much fun that at first Auntie forgot how bad things had been in town. When Wayne Roberts gave them a holler to get back inside, it was too late. Auntie watched in horror as the kids swarmed poor Mr. Roberts.

"Auntie tried to block out his screams with her hands over her ears, but it didn't work. She had to listen as those demon children sucked the life from their dinner. That's all Wayne Roberts had been to them, dinner.

"They walked back to the bandstand after. Auntie said those things didn't spill a drop. Mr. Roberts had been drained yet not a drop touched the ground. Those youngsters were efficient killing machines.

"One of them looked up at Auntie, sitting in her window. She said he grinned up at her. His teeth, even in the darkness, Auntie could see were stained with blood. She could also see the points. Auntie said that boy had teeth like a wolf."

"Did anyone else try to approach them?" Roland asked.

"Mrs. Roberts," Patricia began. "She ran from the house with a scattergun pointed right at those kids. She screamed at her husband to get up and get back inside. When one of the girls walked toward her, poor Mrs. Roberts cried and screamed, over and over, 'No!no!no!' The girl was Jennifer Roberts, her niece.

"When the girl smiled her demon smile at Mrs. Roberts, the gun went off. Mrs. Roberts shot her niece point blank in the face with that gun. The girl's head disappeared, and her body fell to the ground. Black gore spewed out of the thing's neck. Mrs. Roberts just stared at what she had done. She loved that girl. Her husband lay dead on the ground, and her only niece lay at her feet without a head.

"Her grief was so great, she forgot about the rest of them. The woman didn't have time to cry for help. The five demon children descended on her like a pack of wolves. The first one grabbed her by the hair and spun her head so fast and with such force, the poor woman's head came right off. The one who did it held the macabre thing above him so he didn't spill anything. The others covered her fallen torso on the ground.

"Auntie saw them. As plain as day, she said. She knew every one of those boys and girls. At least she knew who they used to be. The things she saw that night were not people anymore."

"What was it about them that makes you say that?" Roland asked.

"The worst is the eyes. The eyes of those things were black. Not just the iris and the pupil. Even the whites of their eyes were black as coal. Their skin lost color, the longer they were d…" She paused. "The longer they were like that."

"Auntie didn't know that when she told me about them. She described the eyes and their pale faces. Through this ordeal, I saw vampires like those, that had only turned a day or so before. They didn't look too different from what they looked like in life. I also saw some who I didn't know, men who surely traveled to Kings Shore with the old one, the monster who began this nightmare and you could see what that existence did to them, their black, expressionless eyes, their pale, thin skin. In the days that followed, I saw the very one who brought this plague upon Kings Shore. His skin was so thin I could see dark veins below the surface."

"What happened after Mrs. Roberts?" Roland asked.

"They ran out of town. They weren't running from anything. Auntie didn't think they were running to anything either. She said it looked like they were just being youngsters, running off to find something fun to do.

"Maybe they left because they had their fill. Maybe they just didn't want to push their luck. After all I've seen, I still don't know if they used reason or just acted on instinct."

"Maybe a combination of both," Roland said. "Did they come back?"

"Not that night, but we hadn't seen the last of them. No, we definitely hadn't seen the last of that lot."

"You look tired, shall I take you home?"

Patricia didn't reply. She looked out over the black water for a moment, then returned to the car.

Chapter 21

It was late as Roland accompanied Patricia inside her home. She sat in her usual spot on the couch. Roland didn't wait for her to ask, he just went into the kitchen and returned with two full glasses of water.

"You're a dear," she said.

She took a dainty sip while he gulped his down without a breath. He wiped his lips with the back of his hand and set the empty glass on the coffee table.

"Can I fix you something to eat?" he asked her.

"That would be nice. I am terribly tired."

He looked down at a different woman than the one who greeted him that first day. Patricia's hands had a slight quiver, and her solid frame had gone stooped and frail looking. Small imperfections had blossomed on her skin that hadn't been there just the day before. This woman had aged more in the past few days than she had in decades.

Roland picked up his glass and returned to the kitchen. He poked around in the fridge and pulled out several items: lettuce, mustard, sliced Swiss and a plate covered with sliced ham. On the counter, he found a bag of rolls, a basket of tomatoes and a dish of butter.

Not quite a half hour later, he emerged from the kitchen and set sandwiches, pickles, carrot sticks and celery spears down in front of his host.

"My lady," he announced. "Dinner is served."

"Good heavens," she said. "You didn't need to make such a fuss. A few crackers and a slice of that cheese would do."

"Let us not forget, I made enough for me too," he said with a boyish smirk.

The two ate in silence. Roland was thankful for that. He didn't think the next chapter of Patricia's life would be very pleasant dinner talk.

She nibbled on one of the sandwiches and the occasional veggie stick, while Roland polished off three of the sandwiches and a handful of carrots and celery spears.

He excused himself to retrieve his refilled glass from the kitchen. When he returned, Patricia announced she could eat no more, and set half of her sandwich on the tray before her.

Roland took the tray back to the kitchen. He put everything back in the fridge that could be saved, scraped the rest into the trash and put the dishes in the sink. He would wash them up after Patricia went to bed.

"That was wonderful, Roland," she said when he sat across from her again.

"Some day you will make a wonderful husband."

"Which brings up a question that begs to be asked," he said. "Why did you never marry?"

"I was engaged in the spring of 1911. His name was Clive Cuthbert. I was to be a June bride the next year. Clive was killed in a logging accident three weeks after he put that ring on my finger. They were clearing a place just over there," she said pointing to the window on the north side of the room.

"Daddy told him he could have fifty acres to start. They would have it cleared by mid-summer and have a modest house built before autumn gave way to the snow. Clive worked day and night on the land. Falling trees, hauling them to the mill and blasting roots kept him away from me for days at a time. He was ten acres into the job when a tree trunk split while he was cutting. No man, no matter how big and strong, is a match for a thousand pounds of falling tree. His body was so damaged, they wouldn't let me see him. I said goodbye through the lid of a coffin, to the only love of my life."

"You never met anyone else?"

"Oh, there were plenty of would-be suitors in the early years. I was a single woman of property," she said. "Many said I was quite a looker in my youth."

"I have no doubt," he said.

She pointed to a picture on the mantel. Roland retrieved it, barking a shin on the coffee table when he returned.

"Watch where you're going, young man."

He handed her the picture and massaged his throbbing leg while she looked at the photo.

Handing it back to him, she said, "That's me and Clive the day he proposed. I have another with Daddy and Mother standing between us."

Roland studied the old picture. Shades of black and gray and white formed a snapshot in time that may well have been the last happy moment in this grand lady's past.

"You were a nice looking couple," Roland said, and he meant it.

Without another word, he walked the photo back to where it belonged. Roland returned it to its place amongst the other Owens family portraits and rejoined her.

"I think," he said, holding out a hand to her, "that it is time for me to get some sleep. May I assist a lovely lady?"

With a smile that went all the way to her eyes, Patricia accepted his offer. She got to her feet and walked him to the front door.

"Until tomorrow then," he said.

"Until tomorrow," she said and closed the door, leaving Roland on the porch.

Chapter 22

As each piece of the story came out of Patricia, it seemed to take a bit of her with it. She slept a lot now, and Roland had started to worry. He pleaded with her to see a doctor, or to let him summon one to her house but she refused. She actually laughed at the notion that Roland could find a doctor that still did house calls.

He again used her sleep time to go over the tapes and type notes about things that might have been said while the recorder wasn't running.

Roland set a glass of lemonade on the side table out on the porch. Over the western horizon, the slightest purple line gave the only hint of the glorious day that had just passed. A stiff breeze came in from the lake, bringing with it a chill air that made Roland glad he had a jacket with him.

Seated on the porch, Roland set his recorder on the table beside his glass and pushed Play. Patricia's voice came from the small device, a bit tinny, and not just a little raspy. The way some old people sound. Roland made a mental note to be more forceful about a doctor.

After some social nattering about how much she appreciated him making her dinner and cleaning up, Roland allowed himself to be pulled right back into the story he was hearing for the second time that night.

We buried those men the next morning. The sun wasn't even high in the sky when their graves were filled in. Their families were moved into the homes of the reverend and the mayor. Just until something else could be arranged, you understand.

After that, the whole town met at the church to decide what to do next. Some wanted to run, and others were too scared to run. As I mentioned, there was only one road out of town, and it was lined with trees for a long way. If the monsters responsible were hiding in the woods, anybody trying to leave would be easy pickings.

I so admired Daddy when he stepped to the pulpit in that church.

"We have to find them," he said. "And when we find them, we have to kill them."

"How?" somebody from the back of the room called out. "How do we kill these things? They may look like men, but I never saw no man fly through the air like that. I never saw no man take two shots in the chest, point blank, and walk away. How do we kill something like that? They can't be killed."

Well, didn't the whole room break into a raucous tirade. It took Daddy at least five minutes to calm them down enough to continue. He held his hands up and motioned for silence, he hollered out, but in the end, he just had to wait them out a bit. Eventually, they did settle down. The roar dulled to a thrum, and the thrum to a buzz. Then, like someone pushed the mute button, the room went quiet. Mother sat beside me, holding my hand. She squeezed it so tight I thought I might never be able to use it again.

The quiet hung in the air for a moment; then, whispers started to fill the void. Before the noise could take over again, Daddy made an announcement.

"I know how to kill them," he said over the din of whispering voices.

"And how do you know how to kill these demons? Have you seen one die?" It was the same man at the back who spoke out earlier. There is always one in the crowd. One who thinks all is lost. I'm sure his first thought before every difficult task was, it will never work. Do you know the type, Roland?

"I do, Patricia," he said, looking down at the recorder. "The network legal department is full of them."

"Not only have I seen one die," Daddy said. He looked so much in charge up there speaking to the town. So handsome. Daddy was a natural born leader, and this town needed someone to lead them. "I have seen two of them die."

He paused to make sure he had all their attention. If Daddy were around today, he would surely have been Prime Minister, if he wanted.

"Not only did I see them die," Daddy said, "I killed them with my own hands."

Well, the room erupted hearing those words. Some calling Daddy a liar, and others wanting to know more. It seemed forever before order was restored. Daddy didn't have a gavel, and he didn't hold his arms in the air to quiet the crowd this time. He just stood there with his hands on his hips waiting for them to have their say. When they did, and the roar had faded to silence again, the man in the back spoke once more.

"Who? Who did you kill, Mr. Rich Man?"

Daddy told them about that night. The night he got home and little Timmy was drawing the very life from my veins. He told them about decapitating the boy and burning his body.

Daddy told them about Bill. The way he hung upside down outside the window.

About taking his head off with the gun. He told them about burning him behind the barn.

I wept aloud when I saw tears running down my father's cheeks as he relived that night.

Bill may have been hired help, but he was Daddy's friend.

"If we remove the head," Daddy yelled, "the body dies."

"Do you think they are going to let us walk right up to them with an axe and cut their heads off?" somebody else called out.

"I didn't say it would be easy. I know it is going to be dangerous. What choices are we left with?" Daddy said.

Of course, Daddy was right. There was no other choice, and they all knew it. The problem was, we didn't have even the slightest idea where they were hiding. If they were in the woods, we could search all day and not cover even a small bit of it.

"How are we going to find them?" Mona Chillson asked Daddy from the front row.

"Mona, I think we have to wait for them to come and find us."

Chapter 23

"Good morning," Roland said as he approached Patricia's front porch.

"Well, look at you," she said. "So casual today. You are taking this vacation thing to heart."

He looked himself over. Walking shorts, golf shirt, ankle socks, and Reeboks. He could pass for a tourist in the Florida Keys without notice.

"Just trying to fit in at the café in town," he said. "I don't know what it is like in the winter, but this morning every table had a family of vacationers."

"I stopped going to town a long time ago. Everybody I knew has been dead for decades. Back then, Kings Shore was a small farming town. Now all the people who live in the cities come here, spend a week, pay $20 for a $5 breakfast and go home unfulfilled."

"Surely some of them have fun here," Roland said.

"Oh, I don't doubt that. Mostly the young ones, who play on the beach. The teenagers who sneak away and drink beer and have sex. I'm sure they will remember it fondly. I believe that for most of the working class, they come to get away from the everyday woes. You can't escape them though, can you? You can go to the other side of the world, but when you get home, you still have to pay the mortgage. For most, they also have to pay for a week's luxury they couldn't afford."

"How long has it been since you have been away from here?" Roland asked.

"Roland," she said, then paused. She seemed to be debating on whether to continue her thought. "I was born in this house. I went to school in St. Thomas church in town. Daddy made his living off the forest of this area. I did likewise, after his passing. I have lived very comfortably off the hard work of others. Been away? Heavens, Roland. I have never been farther than Toronto, for a few business negotiations, and when I was a girl, Mother and I would travel to Toronto with Daddy sometimes when he went there for business."

"With your resources, you could have seen the world." He surprised himself at the incredulous tone in his voice, and it wasn't lost on her.

"I have seen more than any person should. I was born in a time without automobiles. Growing up, there was no television or talking movies. In Kings Shore, there were no movies period. Daddy took me to the pictures in Toronto when I was a girl. That's what we called a movie theatre, the pictures. We entertained ourselves with books. We sat together in the evenings and talked to each other. I witnessed the birth of the automotive age. I saw television take over where the radio once ruled. Now every child on the street has a phone and a computer. I have seen a great deal, wouldn't you say?"

"I would," Roland replied.

"When the fall of 1912 turned the trees every shade of red and yellow, I decided that if I could see one more sunset and one more morning where the hills and forests were covered with new snow that I will have seen everything I wanted to see in life."

She looked at him and smiled at his blank expression.

"Have you ever seen a crocus break through a late snowfall? It is nature saying, 'You can try to stop me, but I am coming anyway.' It truly is something to see. I guess my point is I don't have to see the world because my own little corner of it is beautiful."

"Okay then," he said. "At the town meeting, your father said the strangers would come looking for you all. Is that..."

Patricia giggled, stopping Roland in mid-sentence.

"Something funny?" he said.

"I was just thinking about the uproar at that meeting when Daddy made that statement, everyone hooting and hollering. Of course, no one wanted those men coming back. That's what they called them, those men. Well nobody wanted them coming after them. So they all had something to say about Daddy's plan."

"You said that's what they called them. What would you call them?" Roland asked.

"I guess the short answer, and the one most likely to get me put in the funny farm, is vampires. I personally thought of them as demon spawn. Demons, or vampires, were only the symptom. The disease was much worse."

"I don't understand," he said.

"Those men were just men when they arrived in our lovely hamlet. Unfortunately for them, Mr. and Mrs. Steen moved into the old Adams house."

"The man in that well," Roland said. "He was dead. Had been buried for…"

"Evil never dies," Patricia told him again, as though it weren't getting into his brain.

"We can't blame the Steens though. How could they know? How could anyone know? Even if we knew and warned them, would you have believed a story so wild?"

Roland nodded his head to agree with her. The problem was, he was hearing it now inside his own head. He battled with his own thoughts from the start. His modern mind telling him she was crazy, and his heart telling him she was for real. Finally, Roland believed every word she told him. Hell, the woman was 120 years old, why spin a tale of crap at this point?

Chapter 24

Roland sat beside Patricia on the porch swing. A cold front had moved in overnight ushering in rain and a cool breeze. The roof over the veranda kept the drizzle off them, but they both held their teacups to keep warmth in their fingers.

Moisture from the air collected on the bottom of the gutters and dripped rhythmically on the scraggly rosebush at the base of the porch. You'd think with the way the extra water dripped on that bush it would thrive, but the evil in the ground where old Bill expired refused to release the pathetic shrub.

Patricia put her journal on the side table and pulled her sweater close at the neck.

"Was that the only good thing you could write about that day?" Roland asked.

She gave a nod, then looked out across the road.

"They came in the night, just like Daddy said they would,' she began. "Somehow those bastards, the men who had gone missing, found the families they left behind in the lives they lived two days before. The mayor and his wife were found like the Wilson boy, drained and grey. The family they took in had disappeared. Same thing over at the reverend's place. Some tried to say those women did it and ran off with their children. Can you imagine? Women killing the people who took them in and running off in the night with those things out there in the woods."

Roland could imagine people saying just about anything under that kind of strain. He said, "They were frightened and tried to comfort themselves with a tale that made it easier to sleep at night."

Patricia shrugged and continued.

"By the time we arrived in town, we found a bunch of beaten men. Their faces had no anger, only fear and defeat. There should have been outrage, but they all looked like lame deer, separated from the herd and surrounded by wolves. They had accepted their fate and were praying it would be over without too much suffering. I think Daddy was angered more by that than he was the death of his friends."

"What did he do to rally the troops?" Roland asked.

"They were beyond pep talks. Daddy told them that the only way to prevent the mayor, the reverend, and their families from turning into the same monsters as those responsible for their deaths was to cut off their heads and burn the bodies."

"I'm sure that didn't make him very popular," Roland said.

"It didn't," she agreed. "Not a single man would help him. He didn't want me to help, but he could not do it all alone. We went in those houses, just me and my father. We dragged the corpses of people we knew and cared for out into the street. We loaded them on our wagon and took them to the cemetery. Daddy did convince the undertaker to get the graves dug at least. Once that was done, more men joined in, and when it was time to do the worst of it, Daddy didn't need me to help. They carried each body to a grave. Daddy took his axe from the wagon, walked over to the reverend, and before anyone could object swung that blade down on the reverend's neck. His head rolled into the hole, and Daddy crossed himself before bending, asking the reverend's forgiveness, and rolled his body in too.

"My 'bigger than life' father stood beside that hole and wept. I wanted to go to him, to hold him, but someone held me back. I never knew who held me until later. It was Mother. She had not wanted to go anywhere near town, but in the end, she couldn't stay away."

"I'm sure it meant the world to you and your father that she was there," Roland added.

Patricia nodded, sipped her tea, and closed her eyes.

"Daddy asked one of the men at his side to fetch the container from our wagon. It was a can of kerosene. He poured some into the grave, tossed in a match and walked away.

"Flames spewed out of the ground like a volcano. Once the initial kerosene burned off, acrid black smoke rose from the hole.

"Oh, the smell," she said, waving her hand in front of her nose in an attempt to fan the offending odor away. "As soon as the swirling breeze churned that smoke around, people began to vomit. The stink from that fire made everyone sick. We didn't all vomit, but everyone felt like they might.

"The other bodies were treated the same. Daddy didn't have to do it alone with the rest. The other men all pitched in."

"He led by example, and they followed," Roland said.

She nodded, and holding her hand out, said, "Roland, dear, help an old woman to her feet. I think it's time we had some lunch."

Chapter 25

After lunch, Patricia excused herself and went to lie down. Roland planned to be more forceful in his efforts to get her to see a doctor. He remembered thinking Patricia looked to be a young eighty, younger even. Now he thought she looked terribly old and tired. A sudden slide like that couldn't be good.

While she slept, Roland went for a walk. He followed the same path he had taken with Patricia the day they went to the cemetery. Without Patricia to slow him down, it took no time at all to get there.

He took more time reading headstones. Names from Patricia's stories appeared before him on one marker after another. Sadness fell over him as he read names of people with whom he was beginning to feel a kinship. Like reading a good book, Roland had gotten attached to the characters. The problem here, these characters all died during the telling of her story.

Men with wives, women with children, and children with a whole life ahead of them did not make it out of the summer of 1912.

He made a mental note to return with his computer and do a detailed map of each site, with names and dates. Then he walked back to the road.

He planned on going straight back to Patricia's. The rain had stopped, and the sun managed to burn off most of the cloud cover, chasing away the cool breeze and leaving behind warmth and humidity. The shade of her porch swing became more appealing as he broke a sweat.

Roland walked in a daze, covering ground but unaware of his progress.

When he got to the path that led to the well, he left the road without really choosing to. He staggered, zombie-like, to the ruined old farm. He gave the rubble of the building a wide berth until the old well came into view.

The long grass, still damp from the morning's rain, soaked his jeans to the knees. The warm, humid air, combined with the stress of being back at the well, had his shirt equally wet beneath his arms.

The barren ground around the well had grown. He was sure the ring of dead earth around the stone had doubled in size, maybe more. He could feel an energy coming from beneath the rock that covered the opening, and shuffled back, putting more space between himself and the evil that lived there.

He was sure of it now. Evil lived beneath that stone. He could now feel deep inside himself what Patricia had been trying to tell him. Evil never dies, not ever.

War waged within him. A force pulled him toward the rock, and self-preservation pushed him away. It was a tug-o-war, and Roland Millhouse was the rope.

His stomach began to roil, and his head to swoon. Roland knew if he didn't break free from the pull of the demon beneath the surface, he might be consumed by it. Despair within him grew so great that he contemplated suicide just to end the grief.

He turned and ran. He ran as fast as his shaky legs would carry him. He didn't stop until his lungs were on fire and his legs were unable to support his weight. He staggered to the grass about five hundred yards from Patricia's driveway.

He fell down on all fours, his chest heaving in vain attempts to recover from the over-exertion. Nausea built in his gut, and it took every bit of the minimal strength he had left to fight off the urge to vomit.

When the nausea passed, and Roland's breathing slowed to something almost manageable, he allowed himself to fall over on his side. He rolled onto his back and lay in the grass, knees bent, eyes closed, taking deep breaths, in through the nose, out through the mouth. In through the nose, out through the mouth.

When Roland opened his eyes, it was dark. He couldn't remember ever falling asleep like this. The run must have taken more out of him than he knew. He stood and looked around. The road looked so different in the dark. The trees seemed to be closer to the road, and so much bigger.

He remembered being close enough to Patricia's house to see it when he collapsed from exhaustion. Now all he could see was the road and the trees. After all he had heard in recent days, Roland didn't like being out here after dark, and he started to walk in the direction he knew the old woman's house to be.

He walked further than he thought necessary, and still saw only trees and road. Roland began to jog until he heard a noise in the trees. It sounded like the snap of a fallen branch being stepped on. He stared in the direction of the noise. When he was sure there was nothing there, he continued up the road, no longer jogging, but not walking at a leisurely pace either.

He saw a pair of red lights ahead and assumed it was a car leaving Patricia's.

"Who would be leaving her house?" Roland asked himself. "I have been here a week, and she hasn't had a single visitor."

He concentrated on the tail-lights as he continued to walk. The car must be parked, the lights should have disappeared into the distance.

"What the…" he began. Before he could finish, he realized the lights weren't lights at all. It was a man, and the red glow came from his eyes. Roland stopped walking so suddenly, he almost fell forward. He wanted to turn and run, but his feet wouldn't obey his commands. In seconds, the red eyes closed the gap, and Roland understood what Patricia meant about evil. It was no longer an abstract concept. Evil lived and breathed and had a shape.

The demon's arm flew up faster than Roland could see, cupping its talon-like hand around the base of Roland's neck and pulling him in.

It sunk its long fangs into Roland's throat and a torrent of red life flowed from the wound.

Roland screamed, and the scream woke him to a glorious sunny afternoon.

Chapter 26

"You look like hell, young man," Patricia said as Roland made his way to the front porch.

His normally perfect hair flared out in every direction, his shirt hung over his right hip, while the left side was still partially tucked. Bits of dried grass clung to his clothes, and his eyes were very close to vacant.

Her greeting brought a weak smile to Roland's face. The thought of Patricia, who had aged decades in the past week, telling him he didn't look good was cute.

"I think your stories may be taking a toll," he said.

"Do tell."

"I went for a walk while you were resting. I went back to the cemetery, and…"

"You stay away from that well," Patricia warned. "Do you hear me?" She scolded him in a way a mother might a child to keep him safe from known danger. Patricia told her tales with strength and determination. The only emotions she had displayed during the telling were love for those she'd lost, and sadness for the unspeakable waste of it all.

Now, her wide-eyed stare and stern tone showed Roland an emotion he didn't think Patricia capable of. Fear had come to Kings Shore, and Patricia found it.

Roland stepped back, as though some of that evil she claimed to be hosting would at any time flare out of those terror-laden eyes and burn into his own like lasers.

"It's getting bigger," he told her, his voice quivering. "The dead ground that surrounds the well, I mean. I think it's twice the size it was the last time I saw it."

"Promise me you will not go back there. I showed it to you because I thought it important for you to see, but nobody should go near there."

There was no mistaking the serious expression on the old woman's face. That place was evil and dangerous. Roland believed it even though he tried to convince himself otherwise. Did Patricia believe true evil lurked beneath that rock? Absolutely.

Did Roland believe that place should be fenced off to prevent anyone from accidentally stumbling onto it? Without a doubt.

"You don't have to worry about me," Roland said. "If I live to be 120, I hope to never feel the pull of that place again. It felt like…"

"Like the happiness was being sucked right out of your soul?" she asked.

"Exactly," he answered, nodding.

"Are you well enough to continue?" Patricia asked him.

It wasn't until then that he noticed the always-present journal on her lap. Roland didn't feel at all like listening to more of this tale of horror, but he needed to know more just as much as he feared to hear it. He sat in the chair next to her and motioned to the book.

Patricia's Journal—Saturday, June 22, 1912

We are going into town tonight. Daddy is convinced that we will be safer if we all meet at the church and confront the monsters together.

God be with us.

"When we arrived at the church, only a few of the farmers and loggers were there. Daddy was sure the others were not coming," Patricia began. "He thought they had decided to hold up where they were. He was right about some, but before the sun fell below the horizon, the church filled up. Farmers, loggers, and townfolk all squeezed into that small church."

"Not all of them came, though, did they?" Roland said.

"Not all," she agreed. "We waited and watched from the doors and windows. The moon was only half that night, and the stars were blocked by a few clouds, but the men had set bonfires and put lanterns around the church. If those demons came, we would see them.

"It was so hot in that church. Too many people, and no breeze to move the air. Of course, even if it was windy that night, with the windows and doors closed, it would have done us no good.

"I remember thinking cruel thoughts about some of those people. The smell of them made it hard for me to breathe. It was a church, and most Sunday's everyone was bathed and dressed in their best. That night many of the men had come directly from a hard day's work. When a man works hard in the field, or the mill, or cutting in the woods, he works up a smell. Close up a bunch of those men in an old church and, well I think you get my meaning.

"Just when I thought I could take no more." She paused. "I wasn't the only one you know. Who was feeling antsy in there, I mean. With the heat, and the smell, and the stress of what might be upon us, everybody in the church felt the same to some degree."

"I can't imagine anyone who wasn't feeling it," Roland said. "I feel it now, just listening to your story. Did anything happen that night?"

"They came," she said. "The two strangers and all the people who were unaccounted for. They walked right down the center of the road. Somebody whispered, 'Here they come.' Some crammed themselves around the windows to get a peek. Others hugged each other. Many prayed or cried. I held Mother, while Daddy tried to get a look through the window."

"Did he?" Roland asked. "Get a look at them I mean."

"Oh, he saw them alright. Those things walked right up to the front of the church. Daddy said they stood there, staring at the door. Those abominations made no attempt to get in. They just stood there in the street, right out front. One of the women in the church saw her brother out there. At least she saw what was once her brother. She screamed at him to come inside. Said we could protect him from those evil men. He didn't even look in her direction. That woman begged some of the men to go out there and bring her brother inside, but none would."

CHapter 27

"Can you guess what our next problem was?" Patricia said.

Roland shrugged and shook his head.

"We had most of the town in that church. Those demons were outside."

"I see," he said.

"If anyone left, they risked attack from the monsters. The church was perfectly suited for that many people to sit for an hour-long sermon, but it was definitely not roomy enough for sleeping. There were small children in there, and they were getting very cranky."

"I'm not surprised," he said. "I remember my mother scolding me every Sunday for fidgeting during mass."

"It seemed the creatures could read the mood inside. They turned and walked out of town. Some thought it was a trap, and others felt those things had just gotten bored. Either way, we were in a dilemma. We couldn't stay in the church all night, and it wasn't safe to leave."

"I'm guessing that eventually, nature would win out over fear," Roland said. "After all, I'm guessing a church from a hundred years ago didn't have indoor plumbing."

"You're right about that. That old thing didn't even have an outhouse. Shortly after the monsters left most everyone in the church needed to relieve themselves. I'm sure nerves had something to do with it. The closest toilet was about a half mile away. It was decided to go in groups. The first group consisted of two men, two women, and three children."

"Were they armed?" Roland asked.

"The men were. They left the church and began the walk to the Connelly house. Ben Connelly led the group. He volunteered his house since it was the closest toilet to the church. We watched them from the windows, and some of the men left in the church had the rifles ready to shoot if anything happened.

"Arthur Taylor followed the group with the women and children in the middle. They walked with a purpose, Ben and Arthur looking every which way, like they were watching a tennis match. Of course, they were looking for those monsters.

"They got almost all the way to Ben's house before they began to relax. You could see their gait change. The men stopped looking around, and the women released the children's hands and let them walk along untethered. One of the children wandered away from his mother. He went a few strides toward the shadows at the edge of the street. I think they all felt the threat had left when the strangers walked out of town. That was why the child's mother let him wander.

"They could not have been more wrong. The boy vanished. Those things can move faster than the eye can see. Almost that fast anyway. One of them snatched that child into the shadows. His mother, Emma I think her name was, ran after the boy. Ben and Arthur trained their weapons at the darkness.

"While they watched the woman chase after her boy, both of them were grabbed. We didn't see the creatures until they seized Ben and Arthur from behind. Both rifles fired when they were attacked. Poor Emma was hit. The shot took the right side of her head clean off. She went down in a heap. One of her legs went into a spasm, like she was having a fit. The rest of her didn't move."

"Jesus," Roland uttered, his head shaking back and forth as if he could stop the ancient event from happening through sheer will.

"The things almost released Ben and Arthur when Emma went down. I think the sight of all that blood pouring from the woman's head distracted them. One of the men in the church fired at them. It would have been a difficult shot for a professionally trained marksman. Pete Muldoon was a decent shot, but he wasn't up to that. His bullet struck Ben in the shoulder. The demons went into a frenzy. They both bit fatal wounds in the throats of their prey. Blood sprayed out in pulsing streams. And those things, those…"

"Vampires," Roland said, trying to fill in her statement.

Patricia nodded. "Vampires. They lapped it up with relish. Linda Ferry, the other woman in the group, grabbed up her daughter and ran back to the church. The other child, Emma's little girl, walked over to her mother. That leg still twitched, and even from the church. I could see the blood pooling around her.

"Another vampire thing appeared, standing over the child. Three shots rang out from the church. They were trying to protect the little girl. Two rounds found their target, and the vampire near the girl staggered. Dark stains began to blossom on the thing's shirt. It bared its teeth at us. I will not forget those teeth. They were like wolf fangs, long and gleaming in the light from the bonfires. He grabbed the child. Oh, Roland, how that baby screamed. The thing holding her looked back at us and smiled. Then he sank those fangs into that child.

"She didn't fight him," Patricia said. "Well, a little when he first picked her up, but he stroked her face, and the child calmed right away. When he bit down on her neck, she went rigid for a second, then relaxed, and that demon drained her. There was nothing anyone could do. If we went outside, we would have been next.

"When the child had nothing more to give, that thing threw her into the dirt like she was a piece of rubbish. I couldn't look away. I was repulsed by the vision, but powerless to avert my gaze.

"Ben and Arthur were also left in the dirt as the three vampires walked back into the woods, leaving the four bodies behind."

"What about the Ferry woman and her daughter?" Roland asked.

"They got back to the church. A man at the door, I can't remember who, refused to open it. Daddy went to the door, knocked the coward aside and let Linda in. Poor woman was so scared she wet herself. She carried her child as far from the church door as possible and vomited."

Chapter 28

Roland went to the kitchen. As usual, Patricia had set out a tray. On the tray were glasses, a plate of chocolate chip cookies and a pitcher of something red.

The ice clinked against the crystal side of the pitcher as he carried it to the porch. He set the tray on the table between their chairs and filled two glasses.

"Wild-berry punch," she said with a smile.

"My favorite combination," he quipped. "Wild-berry punch and chocolate chip cookies."

"Yours too?"

He raised his drink to her. They clinked glasses, and they both sipped.

"So, you have an overcrowded church, no plumbing, and homicidal vampires," Roland said, raising a finger to count off each point. "What happened next?"

"Daddy took charge again. I could see the tired look in his eyes. He wanted somebody else to take the lead, but nobody did.

"'I counted three,' Daddy called out to the men around him. 'Is that right?'

"He got some nods, and a few answered with a 'yep' or 'uh huh.'

"'Okay, it's like I told some of you earlier, to kill them you have to take off their heads. A shot to the chest hurts them, but it doesn't stop them."

"'Just how do we do that?' someone called out.

"'Scatterguns. A load of buckshot will do it, but you have to let them get close. How many scatter guns do we have? Hold 'em up, let's see."

"They did what they were told," Patricia said. "Five guns were held high. Daddy counted them out, then asked for four volunteers to go out with him. I put my hand up right away."

"I would have been surprised if you hadn't," Roland said. "They didn't let you go, did they?"

"Daddy said only men could go. A few men started to raise their hands, only to have their wife pull it back down. It took Daddy some time to convince everyone that this was something we had to do.

"Some said he should go out there alone. They said it was his fault everyone was stuck in the church in the first place. I wanted to go right over there and slap them that said that. Of course, that part was true. What wasn't said was how defenseless these people would be isolated out on their farms.

"So, five men exited the church. They walked quickly, Daddy leading the way to the three bodies. He checked each one, then looked back over his shoulder to the church. He didn't say anything or make any gestures, but I knew from the slump in his shoulders that there was no hope for those poor people." She took another of her pauses. Looking away over the horizon, she took another sip of wild berry punch, then wiped her lips with the back of her hand.

"A moose wandered out of the trees just then," Patricia said. "Oscar Rivers spun at the sound of it and fired both barrels at the dumb animal. It gave such a squeal, then turned and ran back to the trees."

"Wrong place at the wrong time," Roland said.

"I fear the moose ran into something worse than a load of buckshot when he got into the trees. There was a ruckus in the trees, then that moose fell into the middle of the road. Those monsters killed it and flung it through the air. It wasn't the biggest moose I have seen, but it was an adult. Do you have any idea how much an adult moose weighs, Roland?"

He shook his head. Each chapter of this tale was beyond belief, so why not a flying moose.

"I don't know for sure, but I think the bleeding moose sent those things into hysterics. One of them ran out and grabbed Oscar from behind, and bit down on his neck. Oscar's gun was empty. At first, he tried using it as a club, as the others watched in horror. They couldn't shoot without hitting Oscar, after all.

"Do you know, Roland. Oscar stopped fighting shortly after the initial bite. He just stood there, almost like it was pleasant.

"Fred Drummond was the first to overcome his horror. He walked up to Oscar and point blank fired his scattergun at the thing's head. It was so rapt with Oscar's blood it didn't notice Fred until it was too late. It fell to the ground, most of its head was gone. The legs and arms were still flopping around, but to no purpose.

"Oscar didn't even flinch from the thunderous report just inches from his ear. He just swooned in place, as blood streamed down the side of his neck. Fred tried to talk to him, but he was gone. His mind, I mean.

"Daddy pushed his hanky against the wound, took Oscar's hand and pushed it against the hanky. When Daddy released Oscar's hand, it stayed put.

"I think Fred really angered them when he killed one of their own. We heard human screams of pain from the woods. It sounded like anger, not sorrow. I don't think they felt that way about each other.

"One of the men, a young man I didn't know, panicked and ran for the church. Like a blur, one of the vampires grabbed him and dragged him into the woods. He was too far away for the others to help. Daddy took Oscar by the arm and began to lead him back toward us. Fred picked up Oscar's gun, and they all made their way back toward the church."

Chapter 29

A tear rolled down Patricia's cheek. She didn't try to hide it, or to apologize for her emotional display.

"I am feeling a bit tired," Roland said, sensing she could use a break. He feigned a yawn to give her an excuse to postpone the next piece of this nightmare. "The old well may have taken a bigger toll on me than I realized."

Patricia wiped her tear away with a tissue she produced from the pocket of her slacks. "You do look tired," she said. "I think I would like to listen to some music for a while. It calms me, you know. Sometimes when I think about those dark days, and I feel I may never be happy again, I listen to Sinatra, or Dino, and I feel much better."

"Dino?" Roland asked.

"Dean Martin, child. Surely you have heard of Dean Martin. His voice is like velvet. I saw him in movies. Well, I have to tell you he wasn't much on the screen but he sure could sing."

"If you say so," he agreed. "I don't know if I have ever heard him."

Patricia just stood and went into the house. Just before the door closed behind her, she said, "You stay away from that well, boy."

Roland retrieved his recorder from the table next to the tray. He slugged back the rest of the mixed berry punch from his glass, plucked a cookie from the tray and trundled down the steps to his car.

He gobbled the cookie down, realized that he hadn't eaten since break-fast and decided the first thing he would do was get some lunch or dinner. The sun was still bright and high in the sky, but at this time of year, that didn't mean it was midday.

Roland got in his car, and before he could stop himself, he pulled into the gate at the old cemetery. He took his computer with him and began to catalogue the names and dates on the headstones.

When he got to the big marker, with Owens, Robert, and Louise, Roland paused. He did some math in his head and was sure that Robert Owens did not live through that night the town's people took shelter in the church.

He walked from grave to grave, typing in names and dates. He also took pictures of the headstones.

"Jesus Christ," he hissed. "What the hell happened in this town, and why is there no record of it?"

Roland put his computer and camera on the passenger seat of the car. He reached in to get a bottle of water from the cup holder and chugged it down. He grimaced at the warm liquid, twisted the lid back on and tossed the empty on the seat with his computer.

"Roland," a voice called.

It sounded like a whisper. He couldn't tell if it was male or female. He didn't know where it came from or who said it.

"Who's there?" he called.

He heard no response. He closed the door, walked around to the driver's side of the car and reached for the door.

"Roland," he heard again.

He looked to the source of the voice. It appeared to be coming from the opposite side of the road, and back in the direction of the old woman's house.

No, he realized. The voice was coming from the direction of the old well. He didn't know how he knew that. He knew that a whisper could not be heard from that well, it was too far away. He knew those things, but what he knew with absolute certainty was the well wanted him.

Roland got into his car and drove into town for something to eat. Patricia didn't have to be there to tell him that going to the well would be a bad thing.

Chapter 30

Roland sat across from Patricia at the kitchen table. His eyes had the look of a man who hadn't slept in days. Small veins tracked prominently, etching a path toward the iris. Shadows beneath the lower lids appeared tattooed there. He was dressed in a wrinkled t-shirt and jeans. The television reporter polish that Roland had when he walked up Patricia's driveway a few days prior looked tarnished or gone altogether.

Patricia continued to age exponentially with each passing day. Her cheeks drooped, and her color had turned yellow. Whatever presence living within her memories waged a war against the teller of those memories, and the one-man audience looked to be collateral damage.

On the long oak table, a basket of muffins sat untouched. Roland had poured them both a glass of OJ from the crystal pitcher that followed them everywhere Patricia decided to sit.

"I watched with some relief when they started back to the church," Patricia began. "In a few moments, Daddy would be safe inside with us. At least that is what I thought, that inside the church it would be safe."

Roland reached for a muffin. Patricia slid a small plate to him. He pulled the muffin apart, set the top on the plate, peeled the paper off the bottom, twisted a chunk free and nibbled at it.

"I always eat the bottom first as well," Patricia said.

He smiled. "I have always saved the best for last."

She nodded and sipped from her glass.

"For some naive reason, we all felt safe inside that building. The damn thing was made of wood, and there were bonfires all along the street. A few burning logs tossed on the roof of that church would have had us all running into the street."

"Is that what happened?" Roland asked.

"It seems they had some fear of the church, or maybe what the church represented. The bastards didn't come closer than standing out front."

"Is all that crap in the movies about vampires true?" Roland asked. He was completely serious. Maybe in the weeks or months to come, he would come to look at these stories as the ramblings of an old woman. It was one hundred years ago. Having several deaths in a short span of time could be the result of a bug that could easily be cured with a course of antibiotics today.

This wasn't in the days or weeks to come, however. Roland believed every word he heard from this old woman.

"I have watched them all," she said. "Most people don't believe that I watch them, but I can't help it. Most of what is in those movies is bunk. A few things seem to be accurate, but I think it is more by accident than anything."

"For instance?" he asked.

"They do fear the church. It doesn't hurt them or burn their skin if they touch a cross. It is like a phobia to them."

"That is odd isn't it?" he said. "Phobias are not contagious."

"These things absorb a bit of whatever they feed on. If they drain the blood from a deer, they might improve their hearing or speed. If in desperation they ate spiders, maybe they would find themselves climbing walls."

"Could they turn into bats, if they fed on them?"

Patricia guffawed, uncontrollably. Red flushes rose up in Roland's cheeks, and he could feel his ears warming. Patricia laughed, and it brought back some of the color to her features.

Roland chuckled a bit, which heightened Patricia's enthusiastic chortling. This sent him off, and together they laughed like children with no worries in the world.

"No," she said through her fading chuckles. "They remained the shape of men and women. They took on a devilish ugliness as time passed. Their skin grew taut and pale. Their eyes turned the color of blood or blackened orbs. Their hair went dry and wispy. Even the mildest breeze sent it flittering around their heads. Ugly things."

"But no flying," he said, still laughing.

She turned serious, like flipping a switch. Roland intuited her reaction, and his face went stiff and attentive.

"They can't fly, but the way they jumped it seemed like they could. They could jump so high and fast that you might think they flew away, only to find them standing right behind you. They could also jump from great heights and not be injured.

"That is what happened that night in front of the church. Daddy and Fred were leading Oscar back when one of them landed right in Daddy's path. Daddy's reaction was immediate. He unloaded his gun in the thing's face. The head exploded, a black mist sprayed out behind it, and the thing's body fell to the ground. Fred began to run for the door, dragging Oscar, and Daddy did the same."

Roland looked on with amazement as she stared up to the ceiling with what he thought was a look of admiration. It was as though she had seen this all happen last night. She adored her father, and his last dash for shelter, hauling the bleeding and traumatized Oscar, was heroic.

"Two more landed directly in their path," she said. "Their guns were spent, and they were too far from the church for the guns inside to be of use. Daddy and Fred let go of Oscar and swung their guns like clubs. They should have reloaded after shooting, but hindsight is always clearer, isn't it?"

"Are you up to a stroll around the yard?" Roland asked. He could see that she needed a break. He had developed a liking for Robert Owens. Taking a bit of a break to delay his inevitable demise seemed about right.

"That sounds wonderful," she said. "Why don't you wait on the porch while I get my wrap."

Chapter 31

Roland stood at the foot of the steps, basking in the sun. The house held the cool night air, while the sun had warmed the outside and filled the day with color and life. The Bimmer sparkled in the sun's glow, and every blade of grass and leaf on the trees leaned toward the source of the rays to soak up the energy it gave.

"It is lovely, isn't it?" Patricia said, walking out onto the porch. "The winters here are bitter, but one day like this will erase the memory of a whole winter. Wouldn't you say so, Roland?"

"It really doesn't get better," he said.

She held her hand out. "Help an old woman down would you, dear."

Obediently, he skipped up to the top step and held out his arm. "My lady."

Roland thought she was just being playful until he felt her effort through his arm. Her fingers dug into his skin as she made her way down each step.

She paused at the bottom, took a deep breath, then took her tentative steps along the driveway, her hand still clinging to Roland's elbow.

"I used to walk like this with Daddy. He would hold his arms out like a rooster, showing off to the hens. Mother would take one, and I the other. On a day like this, we would walk for miles. He was like a groom at a wedding. Step, pause, step, pause. Daddy used to walk very fast, you see, so he had to adjust his walk for us women."

"It sounds like a Norman Rockwell moment," Roland said.

"That is a perfect way to describe it." She beamed. Roland could see the glow in her eyes when she spoke of her father. It saddened him all the more to know what was coming next in her tale of horror.

"Mother was on my arm like this when it happened," Patricia said, her monotone voice void of feeling. She had no expression. She only stared straight ahead, her tiny strides moving them along in near slow motion.

"I hadn't even noticed Mother there with me. I watched in terror while things went to hell. You can't kill those things with a whack in the head. Neither gun found its target anyway. They were wicked fast with super-human strength. They blocked the blows with ease. In a flash, both guns were torn from Daddy and Fred's hands. The things just tossed them into the street."

Roland placed his free hand over the hand holding his arm. Her hand was cold, and her voice quivered.

"Are you cold?" Roland asked.

She didn't answer.

"The demons struck Daddy and Fred in the chest. It was surreal to see two men, big and strong and full of life, sent flying from their feet by a seemingly mild blow. They both fell to the street, tumbling and rolling.

"I think that is when I realized Mother had hold of me. I screamed, and Mother screamed. She clamped down on my arm so tight she left a mark. It took a week for that mark to fade.

"While Daddy and Fred were on the ground, both of those things grabbed poor Oscar. He didn't cry out or fight back. Oscar stood still while those things drained him dry. When he had nothing left to give, they released him, and he fell to the road. They were just steps from one of those fires, and we could see Oscar's lifeless eyes staring at us as if to say, 'Why didn't you help me?'"

She stopped walking, retrieved a hanky from her pocket and dabbed a tear from her cheek.

"Silly, isn't it," she said. "Tears for a man who died a hundred years ago. A man I only knew to say good morning to, no more."

"It isn't silly at all, Patricia," Roland soothed.

She walked along in silence for a while. Roland knew she was trying to build up the courage to tell the next part. If remembering Oscar's demise brought a tear, he didn't know how she would get through Robert Owens' passing.

"Well," she said after a while. "There's my bench."

"And not a moment too soon," Roland said. "I could use a rest."

Patricia wasn't fooled and patted his hand.

Roland helped her to her seat and settled down beside her. Her breathing came quick and shallow. She sat quietly, holding Roland's hand until she caught her breath.

Chapter 32

They sat on her bench. Roland held her hand like he was her adoring child. The sun was high in the cloudless sky. A slight breeze sent the long grass at the edge of the road to sway in waves of green.

"The things disappeared after Oscar expired. It was like they got their fill and went home. I forced my way to the door and pushed it open. I screamed at Daddy to get inside. I took a step toward them, and some-one pulled me back in.

'Help them,' I screamed. 'Somebody help them.'

"Two men carrying six-shooters ran into the street. The monsters had fooled us again. Three more vampires dropped from the sky. It could have been the same ones, I don't know for sure.

"God bless him, one of those men had paid heed to Daddy's instruc-tions. He blasted one of those things in the head, one, two, three times. They aren't immortal. Their bodies were once human, and sustain damage like anyone. The thing didn't die, though. Can you imagine that? Three bullets in the head and it wandered dumbfounded about the street.

"The other fella, he emptied his gun into the chest of the creature be-fore him. Six shots in the chest and that thing walked right up to the man, who stood terrified and confused. While the two monsters fed on him, Daddy and Fred scrambled to their feet and ran as fast as they could toward the church.

"They might have made it, but Fred tripped over the gun he had emptied into that vampire's face while he was feeding on Oscar. Fred went down, and one of them jumped on him. Daddy didn't think, if he had, he probably would have left Fred for the lost cause that he was. Daddy ran over and kicked that thing right on the side of his head. What Daddy hadn't considered was the thing's fangs were deep into the side of Fred's neck. When Daddy kicked it, its head jerked sideways, tearing a hole in Fred's throat. So much blood, so much.

"Daddy backed away from it, and I screamed from inside the church. I screamed for him to run. He did too. He ran like a man on fire. You can't outrun a vampire, Roland. You just can't," she said, shaking her head.

"Before Daddy ran ten steps, two more monsters dropped into the road. They were on him before he knew they were there. I fought my way through the door, but no further. I was held back, while I watched Daddy succumb to the things. I fought and screamed, but those people would not let me help him.

"They took my Daddy away. He wasn't dead. I could see his eyes move."

Patricia cried without restraint. Roland put his arm around her shoulder. He pulled her to him, and let her grieve. After one hundred years of pain, Patricia surrendered to the grief. Time does not heal all wounds. This one festered for a century and still crippled this woman's soul.

"We went back inside the church and locked the doors. I collapsed against the closed door and cried. I accused every single man in there of being a coward. I blamed every man in town who still drew breath for Daddy's passing. It wasn't their fault, but grief isn't rational.

"Mother came to me. She sat beside me, and we cried until grief and exhaustion took us. That old church had a lovely stained-glass window. I woke to a sparkling array of colors streaming through that glass. I found no beauty in the window that morning. I found no joy in the sunrise. I woke mother, and we walked from the church. Neither of us set foot in that building again."

"I can't imagine any of those people would be eager to go back there,"

Roland said.

Patricia dabbed tears from her face. "Many did. Not everyone lost someone that night. For some, God is everything. He was for me, until then. I could forgive Him for taking Daddy from me. I will not, however, forgive any God who permits the devil's seed to walk the earth, preying on the people who worship Him."

"Some people who survived thanked God. Some, like me, blamed Him. Still more held to their faith, trying to convince the grieved that He has a plan.

Whatever the plan was, He would have to finish it without me."

She took one of her pauses before returning her attention to Roland.

"There was one small victory that night, Roland."

"Really, what was that?"

"Some of the folks in the church were awake all night. They stood by the windows and watched. The thing that took three bullets to the head wandered around in circles all night. It stumbled and tripped over fallen men and discarded guns. The damn thing would get right back up and walk around. As soon as the sun cleared the horizon and an unobstructed ray of light fell on it, it began to smolder. It writhed and twisted, and tried to scream, but there wasn't enough of its face left to make a noise. Eventually, it burst into flame and fell to the ground. The flames left nothing behind but a scorched shadow on the ground."

"So that's when you found out that it was completely safe to move around during the day," Roland said.

Chapter 33

Roland walked Patricia to the cemetery after she told the tale of her father's brave last night. She held his arm for support as they traversed the uneven ground. When they arrived at the site of her parents' final resting place, he tried to back away and let her pay her respects alone, but she refused to release his arm.

Patricia stood motionless, looking down at the old granite marker. The names were clearly visible, but the wear of wind and rain had the headstone looking weathered.

"Poor Mother," she said after a few minutes.

Roland placed his left hand over hers, as she clung to his arm. Her hand was so cold. How could anyone's hands be that cold on a day like this?

"She bore up as well as she could, but Mother was a weak woman. Not all women could endure the seclusion of this area the way it was then. She did her best, but once Daddy was gone." She paused. "Once he was gone, and we knew he wouldn't be back, not ever... Well, that was just too much.

"She left a note." Patricia reached into a pocket in her slacks and took out a small white envelope. She handed it to Roland, her eyes never leaving the names of her parents.

Roland removed a brittle, yellowed piece of paper from the envelope and read.

Patricia,

I can't bear to think of him out there with those things. I have gone to bring him back. If I don't see you in the morning, I have found him, and could not return.

I love you, so much.

You are so strong. Just like him.

I hope you know how much he adored you.

Love, Mother

"As soon as I found this, I went to town and recruited everyone I could to search for her. We didn't find her. Eventually, she found us.

"With Mother and Daddy gone, I moved into town. My Aunt Maggie lived in town. She was Daddy's eldest sister. After Uncle Art died, she came to stay with us. She couldn't live out here in the wilderness. That's what she called our place, the wilderness. Daddy set her up with a place in town. She became the bookkeeper for the mill. She had a small office next to the general store, with an apartment above. She thought the town was not much better than wilderness, but she enjoyed the work and eventually made a few friends.

"I walked into her little office, suitcase in hand, and she knew. I didn't have to tell her Mother had gone, she just knew."

Patricia turned from the grave-site. Roland backed around her, and they walked back to the road. The old woman had retreated into herself, and Roland was happy for the quiet. He listened to the wind rustle the leaves and the grass. He marveled at the clarity of the birdsong. He could swear he heard the waves breaking on the beach but knew that couldn't be true. The lake was at least a half mile away.

He expected her to resume her seat on the bench. They had been up for a good long time. She didn't so much as glance at her bench on this day. Patricia Owens walked with her aged but determined gait, past the bench toward her house. She slowed only once. When they drew even with the path leading to the old well, both pedestrians slowed to cast a glance in the direction of the ruined old farm. Roland felt a pull, and Patricia felt his stride veer in the direction of the path. She dug her fingers deeper into the muscle of his forearm, and he followed her away. Away from the pull of the demon that lived beneath the rock.

Chapter 34

By the time Roland led her into the house, Patricia was barely able to walk. He was certain that she had finally written a cheque her old body could not cash. He guided her to the couch where she collapsed. Her chest heaved as she tried to settle her heart.

"Patricia," Roland uttered. He hoped his fear for her health wasn't coming through in his voice. "Should I get a doctor now?"

She shook her head. Patricia took his right hand in hers, patted it with the other and gave a weak smile. He did his best to return the gesture, but Roland was not at all sure Patricia's story would be told to the end. He felt confident that he heard the last she would be able to tell while they walked back to the house.

She tried to speak, but her ragged breathing made the attempt unintelligible. Roland shook his head to indicate he didn't understand. It was as though her inability to speak had transferred to him.

She raised her hand as though holding a glass, and tipped it toward her.

"A drink. You want a drink?"

She grinned, and he leaped into action. He fetched a glass of water from the kitchen and hustled it back to his host, spilling half of it on the floor and the front of his legs.

Patricia sipped the rest until the glass was empty. Her breathing had slowed and the color was returning to her cheeks. It wasn't the youthful glow she had when Roland first met her, but he was happy to see some recovery.

"You scared the crap out of me," he said.

"I might need to have a few more benches put out there," she replied. "Would you be a dear and bring me a pillow and a blanket? I don't think I am ready to get up, and I do want to sleep a bit.'

Roland looked inquiringly until she pointed him to the door opposite the kitchen. He returned with a brown striped afghan and a white pillow.

"Thank you," she said.

He placed the pillow on the couch and Patricia lowered her head until she lay on the couch, her legs still hanging where they'd been when she was sitting upright.

Roland bent and gently lifted the woman's legs to the soft cushions of the couch, then draped the afghan over her. She didn't say anything else, just closed her eyes and passed into a restful sleep.

Roland marveled at how small and fragile she looked in that moment. She had always been small, but only now did he see her as fragile.

Seated in the chair across from her, Roland stuffed earbuds in his ears and pushed the Play button on his recorder. He listened to the scene Patricia described on that walk back from the graveside visit.

While Robert Owens lost his battle with the vampires at the church, the gang of teenage monsters paid a visit to the farm of Curtis and Maureen Davidson. Christopher Davidson, one of the teens, had found his way home.

The Davidsons knew what their boy had become, but knowing and actually seeing it was apparently too much for Maureen. Curtis did his best to restrain his wife and their youngest from going out to see Chris.

Chris was just a couple of years younger than Patricia. When the news circulated about this demonic gang of teenage monsters, Patricia grew morose. She knew all of those kids. They had attended school together.

They were all two or three years behind her, but Kings Shore of 1912 didn't have many teens, so even the ones who lived on the most remote farms attended school in the same room.

Curtis ran to stop his youngest from opening the door and going to his big brother. That was all Maureen needed. Before Curtis could stop her, Maureen slipped by him and, standing on the front stoop, called to Chris.

The boy walked up to her like any obedient son would. Maureen reached to take the boy's hand, and when she did, he smiled. Maureen knew then that she had made a mistake. The boy's jagged teeth sparkled in the light coming from the opened door behind her.

Curtis threw his youngest son to the floor and ran for his wife. He could see those teeth and the boy's demon eyes. He heard the gasp from Maureen as she spun to flee the creature before her.

She wasn't fast enough, however. Chris grabbed her and pulled her to the center of the yard. Curtis watched as his own son shared in taking the life from his beloved wife.

In his mind, Curtis knew it wasn't really Chris, but his eyes betrayed him. He watched the face of the young man he loved more than life feed on the blood of his own mother.

Overcome with horror, Curtis didn't realize that his youngest had followed him. The boy screamed for them to leave his mother alone. Every one of those monsters looked to Curtis and his boy like they were tasty morsels at a holiday feast.

Curtis hustled his boy inside and locked the door. The two of them sat on the couch, the elder holding tight to his gun, and the younger clinging to his daddy's shirtsleeve with one hand, and vigorously sucking the thumb of his other, a habit he had outgrown eight years ago.

Those monsters stayed out there the whole night. Curtis told the people in town that they climbed trees and swung from the branches like monkeys. One of them had taken to jumping up on the roof and then jumping to the ground. Over and over again he jumped up, then down. He would land with the grace of a cat. Then he'd run around for a while, then jump up on the roof again.

One of them led the Davidsons' horse from the barn. The poor animal had terror in its eyes, but it was powerless to resist them. They brought that animal right up to the front steps and swarmed it.

It tried to run off when the first one dug its demon teeth into that muscular neck. That was when the true power of these things became real for Curtis. When that horse tried to run off, one of those kids grabbed hold of its back leg and ripped it off.

The horse fell to the ground, and while the vampire holding the severed leg lapped up the blood that dripped from it, the other four fed on the horse. The one who bit down on the beast's neck never let go until the poor thing was dead. The others latched on to the gaping hole that moments ago was a powerful hindquarter of a workhorse.

According to Curtis Davidson, when they finished the horse, one of those things actually whinnied.

When the sun breached the horizon, Curtis went outside and dragged Maureen's body over to the horse. He then soaked them both with kerosene and set them ablaze. In his barn, he found similar carnage. Every animal in the barn lay dead, with its throat torn out. Two dairy cows, one Black Angus steer, and seven goats.

They left the chickens. They clucked and cackled in the hen house waiting for breakfast while Curtis wandered around the barn trying to figure out how to drag three full-grown cows outside without a horse to pull them.

Deciding to move the goats first, Curtis dragged one after the other to the fire. He gagged the first time he looked at the blackened burning thing that was once Maureen. The black smoke filled the air with a smell that could make even the strongest man retch.

While dragging the third goat from the barn, something buried beneath the straw caught his eye. The sole of a boot protruded from the pile. It was Christopher's boot, and Christopher's foot was still in it.

Infuriated, Curtis dragged his son from the straw pile. When he got the boy out into the open, the thing hissed, jerked his leg free from Curtis' grasp, and burrowed under the straw again.

Curtis tossed a lit match into the straw and fled the barn just in time to hear the screech and several voices. Whether it was his imagination or reality, he didn't know, but he swore he heard Christopher's voice in one of those screams.

Chapter 35

When Roland woke, the afghan he had used to cover Patricia now covered him, at least from his shoulders to his waist. He pushed himself to a seated position, struggling to remember where he was and how he got there.

Standing, Roland stretched and twisted, trying in vain to loosen the kinks that a night on a couch half the length of his body had inflicted.

That was when it struck him. Where he was and why he was there. Patricia over-exerted herself, curled up on the couch and went to sleep. Afraid her health was worse than she let on, he had curled up on the couch across from her. With more than a bit of anxiety, he looked at the couch where he last saw Patricia. It was empty. The white pillow, dented in the middle where the old woman's head had rested, gave the only clue that there had been anybody there.

"Patricia," Roland called toward the kitchen. She didn't answer, and he called again, only much louder.

"I'm not deaf," she answered from behind him.

He spun to see her sitting on a chair in the darkest corner of the room.

The light, however poor, was enough for Roland to see that

she did look much improved over the previous evening. Her wispy white hair had been teased into a tidy set. She dressed in what Roland had come to consider Patricia's style. Dark slacks, a white blouse and some kind of shawl or throw around her shoulders.

"You were sweet to stay with me last night, Roland, but my furniture was sure not meant for a man as tall as you. You truly must feel dreadful."

"I'm not going to lie, I have felt better, Patricia," he answered through a mild chuckle. "How are you feeling?"

"Right as rain," she said. "I've prepared a light breakfast, if you wish. It isn't much, just pastries and fruit. Why don't you freshen up a bit, then meet me in the kitchen."

By the time Roland entered the kitchen, Patricia was sitting at the table with a steaming cup of tea in front of her.

"You've been here enough to know where everything is. Help yourself," she said.

He grabbed a Danish from the tray, gobbling it down with voracious verve.

When he finished, he poured himself a glass of OJ, chugged it down, ate another Danish with a bit more restraint and refilled his glass.

"Sleeping on a tiny couch must be good for the appetite," she said.

Roland raised his glass in her direction, sipped some juice and asked, "What's on the agenda for today?"

"Well, it is a beautiful morning. I thought we might have a sit on the porch."

"I'm in," he said, grabbing a third Danish.

Patricia walked out to the porch after breakfast. Roland insisted she sit and rest while he cleaned up. It didn't take any time at all for him to wash the few plates and glasses. He continued to nibble on strawberries and grapes while he worked.

When he finished, he picked up the serving tray that Patricia had left; on it were a pot of tea, cups, lemon wedges and a flask of honey.

As with previous days, when Roland found his host on the porch, she sat emotionless, looking out over the land, her journal on her lap and her hands resting on it, neatly folded as though in prayer. He placed the tray on the table, filled two teacups, then took his place in the empty seat.

Roland didn't speak. He looked out over the same expanse, wondering what Patricia Owens saw when she went to the place she was now. Did she see what he saw, or was she looking out, not at a place, but at a time?

Roland had finished his first cup of tea and was pouring another when Patricia broke the silence.

"I think we will get a storm today."

Roland looked up at a sky as clear and blue as any he had ever seen. "You really think so?"

"Couldn't say for sure, but we should take a walk before lunch. The afternoon will be a good time to sit inside and chat."

Still looking up at the blue expanse, Roland said, "Whenever you're ready, Patricia."

Patricia's Journal—Sunday, June 30, 1912

I have only Auntie. The rest of my family has been taken by those things. I pray this nightmare ends soon before anyone else has to suffer.

I am an orphan now. God watch over me.

"I rode out to the house that day," Patricia said, placing the ribbon in the pages and closing the book.

"Your mother didn't return?" he asked.

"She did," Patricia said. "I rode my horse to the house that morning. Aunt Maggie didn't want me to, but I told her that the bad things only happened at night.

"She told me to at least find someone to ride out there with. I stopped at the Petersons. My best friend, Carol, agreed to go with me. Carol's husband had gone to the mill at dawn and wasn't expected back until dusk, so she was happy to have some company.

"Carol never looked quite right up on a horse. She was barely taller than a fireplug, and to tell the truth, she was built like one. It's funny when I think about it now. She was quite a plain-looking thing, but her smile could light up a room. Carol took command of the room whenever she entered. She was a storyteller, and we all sat rapt when she began a tale.

"Suffice to say, the ride out to the house had flown by. Carol told one story after another, and before we knew it, we were standing in front of this house."

Patricia's gaze drifted back out over the landscape. Roland sipped his tea, then set the empty cup on the table between them.

"Not all the bad things happened at night did they?" Roland said.

"We tied the horses to the railing right in front of where you sit. I didn't notice the door until I climbed the steps. The door was closed, but not all the way. We probably should have turned right around as soon as we saw that and rode back to town. We should have sent a posse of men to search the house, but like Daddy, I feared nothing."

"I have no doubt about that," Roland said.

"I placed my hand in the middle of that door and pushed it open. The door has seen a century of weather and settling since, but back then it swung quiet and true. Sunlight flooded into the house like an unwelcome guest. I only took two steps inside and stopped, Carol bumping into me. We could feel warmth cozy against our backs from that sunlight. But the front..." She paused, rubbing her arms like she had just taken a chill from a cool damp breeze.

"I felt a chill in the house. I remember wrapping my arms around myself to shield my body from the cold, and I looked to Carol, who was doing likewise. It was dark in the house. All the drapes and curtains were pulled tight. I know I didn't close the place up like that."

Patricia's voice had dropped to a mere whisper. If Roland weren't sitting so close, he'd not have been able to hear her.

"Roland, it was a terrible feeling. I was home, and I was so uncomfortable. I felt like an intruder in my own house. There was no sense of belonging, only cold emptiness. Can you imagine how that was for me? To feel unwelcome here of all places."

Patricia stopped and looked over to her companion as she pulled her throw tight around her shoulders.

"I can't," Roland said. "It must have been terrible, frightening even."

"I shouted out, 'Is anybody here?' No one answered of course. I wanted to run back to my horse. I wanted to go back to town. I didn't though. I remembered how brave Daddy had been, and I would not be weak. I didn't want Carol to see me turn tail and run either."

Patricia wrapped her arms around herself just as she had done so long ago, as though the mere thought of that day had chilled her.

"We began to search the house. There was no knowing how long that door had been ajar. Any manner of animal could have moved in. I didn't think they would. If animals could sense what I felt, they would have been smart and run in the other direction, just like I wanted to do.

"It took no time at all to check all the rooms on the ground floor. We were young and quite fleet of foot." She said that with a wry smile on her lips.

"The sense of foreboding grew as we ascended the stairs to search the bedrooms. With each riser, the temperature dropped. We had no air conditioner, I still don't use one. This old house can get a fair bit warm up there, but cold is what we felt."

Roland watched as she pulled her wrap even tighter around her shoulders. He dabbed the sweat from his brow while Patricia fought off a chill that took hold of her a century ago and held tight to her weary old frame. He swore he saw her shiver just before she adjusted her shawl.

"I went to my room first," she said. "I walked straight for my closet and put on a sweater. I tossed another to Carol. She looked like a child trying on her mother's clothes. I was always much taller than she, so my sweater hung past her hands. I slid the drapes open wide and stood in the warmth of the sun. The warm rays and the brightness gave me strength and courage."

"I think it just helped you summon what was already there, Patricia," Roland said.

"You're sweet," she replied. "Well, I walked across the hall, Carol right on my heels, and pushed the door to Daddy and Mother's room open. I have never felt such joy, only to be crushed with the weight of a life-time of dread, all in a heartbeat."

Roland sat silently while Patricia dabbed a tear welling from the corner of her eye.

"Mother lay on her bed, and Daddy lay beside her. They both lay flat on their backs. Like a pair of corpses. I think Mother hissed when the light from my open window fanned out across the floor to the foot of the bed. I called to them, but they made no other sound. I was certain at that moment that somebody had found them and brought them here to be laid out for a funeral. I thought, while I was riding out of town to get here, whoever had put Mother and Daddy here must have been on his way to fetch me."

"Would you like to take a break? Maybe a walk to the bench?" Roland asked. He could see the toll this part of the story was taking on her. Tears glistened in her eyes. Her hands quivered in her lap.

"You're a dear for asking," she said. She sipped her tea, placed the cup on the tray. "Help an old woman to her feet, Roland."

Roland stood and extended his hands to her. She gripped them and heaved herself up. Her grip was still strong, but Roland felt a fragility beneath that grip.

"When neither of them answered, I whispered, 'Mother? Daddy? Are you awake?' Of course, by then I knew they were not. But, it was easier to hope.

"I could feel Carol place her hand on my shoulder. I think she whispered something to me, but I can't recall what.

"Everything slowed as I made my way from the door to their bedside. I forgot about the chill. Maybe it was the sweater. I think it was sheer terror. I put my hand on Mother's shoulder to shake her awake.

"So cold." Patricia's voice had trailed to a whisper. She tugged at her wrap, pulling it ever tighter around her shoulders.

"I recoiled at the cold. Like one does when a static shock gets you. You know what I mean?"

He nodded but said nothing. Roland knew she was powering through the grief. Patricia needed to tell this story, and he didn't want to deter her.

"I began to shiver like I was trapped outside in an autumn rain without a coat. I needed to feel warmth, so I rushed to the window and pulled those curtains open."

Patricia's hand sprung up to her ears as if a deafening screech were piercing her brain.

"Oh, Roland, their screams. First Daddy, as he was on the window side of the bed. Mother didn't like to be close to the window, she said it was too drafty.

"Mother's screams came right after Daddy's. It was the sun. I looked at them, lying side by side, their hands folded neatly over their waists, not making any effort to shield themselves from what must have been agony. They just screamed."

Patricia seemed to notice then that she was covering her own ears, and she lowered her hands. Her strides were slow and labored. They had only progressed as far as the road. She clung to Roland's arm, and they turned right and walked toward the cemetery.

A blue Chevy Avalanche passed by. The driver slowed a bit, waved, then continued on. Patricia gave a half wave with her free hand and placed it over the one on Roland's arm.

"I'm not sure that bench is close enough for me today," she said.

"I'm sure you'll be fine," Roland said. Just then they passed the point in the road where it curved to the left, and a shiny new bench gleamed in the morning sun.

"How did that get there?" Patricia asked. He thought she was asking herself, more than him.

"Well, I made a few calls. Told some people how it might be nice to have a new bench along here for a certain elderly citizen. Do you know how many of your neighbors wanted to help? There are ten new benches along this road." It was Roland's turn to dab a tear as he saw the humble look of appreciation on Patricia's face.

They sat on the new bench. Patricia wasn't out of breath, but with a huge exhalation, it was obvious she was happy to be seated.

"It's nice," she said.

Roland sat quietly next to her. He was dying for her to continue but knew better than to prod her for this part of the tale.

"I left my journal at the house," she said after a few minutes. "Where did I leave off, young man?"

"The curtains," he answered. "You opened the curtains to your parents' room, and…"

"The screams," she said. "I was completely frozen with fear. Like a school girl, I cowered from the horror. I looked to Carol who was doing the same as me. Her hands covered her ears trying to block the noise. I was sure if the screams didn't stop soon our ears would begin to bleed or we would go completely deaf.

"That was when we met the man who would help Kings Shore end the nightmare decimating it."

"What man?" Roland asked.

"His name was Bernhard Werner. He was a scrawny little man with a blade of a nose, round gold-rimmed glasses, and a terrible scar that ran from the corner of his left eye, all the way to the corner of his square jaw. He had the palest white skin and wispy straw-colored hair.

"Well, he stormed into that room, yanked those curtains closed, and said, 'Girl, just because they are no longer living, does not mean you should torture them.'

"As soon as the curtains were closed, the screaming stopped. It took Bernhard a while to get us settled enough to understand that he was there to help. We were so scared."

Chapter 36

Roland and Patricia agreed to find the rest of the benches another day and made their way back to the house. While she rested on the couch, Roland fixed them a snack of cheese and crackers and lemonade.

"Lunch is served," he said, placing the tray on the coffee table. "I am afraid the presentation is not as appealing as your work."

"It is perfect," she interrupted.

"Well, I aim to please," he said with a bow. Roland looked to the window. "It is a beautiful day, would it be alright if I opened the drapes?"

She gave a nod, and with a motion that was almost ceremonious, Roland pulled the old drapes aside. The rings protested as they grated on the worn wooden curtain rod, filling the room with annoying sound. Almost as brilliant and sudden as a camera flash, sunlight flooded the room causing both occupants to squint and momentarily turn away.

After their eyes had time to adjust to the brightness, Patricia said, "Do sit," motioning him to the seat across from hers. He did, without another word.

"You said, as soon as those windows were covered, the screaming stopped," Roland began after a few moments of quiet.

Patricia looked from the window back to Roland. She closed her eyes for a moment, like she might be trying to puzzle out a math problem in her head, then smiled.

"'Are you the Owens girl?' Bernhard asked me."

Just then a rumble of thunder rolled from far off.

"It sounds like you might have been right about the storm," Roland said.

Patricia shrugged, looked to the window, then back to Roland.

"I assured him I was the Owens girl, and he began to berate us for cruelty. I didn't get an opportunity to explain myself until the little man was out of breath from his endless tirade.

"I stood before him, mad as hell, and scared out of my mind. Grief was crushing me like a pebble beneath a boulder. The last thing I needed was to be scolded like a child. I explained myself to that man at a volume I have not used before or since."

"I just bet you did," Roland said. He couldn't stop the grin that blossomed on his face. He imagined a twenty-year-old Patricia Owens going postal on Herr Werner and the smile turned into a chuckle.

"He let me have my say, then told me we had to get to work. Can you picture the gall, strolling into my house, uninvited, and telling me I have work to do?

"I stood right in front of him and demanded some answers. Who are you? What are you doing here? Where did you come from? How did you get in?"

"Your father was right," Bernhard said.

"You know Daddy?" I asked. I was quiet then. When he mentioned Daddy, I calmed down.

"I knew him, yes," he replied. He looked to the bed then back to me.

"It was your father who summoned me here. He sent word the day he returned home. He told me of the boy who very nearly ended your life."

"His gaze traveled to my throat. He wanted to be sure there were no fresh wounds from..." She paused.

"From vampire bites?" Roland asked.

She nodded. "Yes, he wanted to make sure I wasn't some kind of food source to those demons."

"Your father told me you were a force of nature," Bernhard said. "I see you may just be that and more."

"You can say that again," Carol said, finally waking from her shock brought on by the screaming.

"Who is this?" Bernhard asked.

"I introduced Carol," Patricia went on. "There was a brief moment of casual nonsense, and Bernhard took charge of the house."

"We must destroy them before the sun sinks below the horizon," Bernhard said.

"Destroy them?" I shouted. "That is my mother and father, not some rabid dog.

What makes you think you can come into our house and make these demands?"

"In 1880, when I was not much more than a boy, the village in Germany where I was born had the same plague that inflicts this place," Bernhard answered.

"We had heard rumors from far across Europe, so when the attacks began, we were not taken completely by surprise as is the case here. Every man and boy child more than ten years of age hunted those things until the scourge had been erased from existence.

"I never would have thought they would be able to make the journey across the ocean. That is why I came to this country. I believed I would never encounter them here.

"Now they are here, and no one will be safe until they are gone. Your mother and father are not sleeping in that bed. If we don't do what needs to be done, they will walk the earth tonight, and if they encounter you, they will take your life without remorse."

"I knew he was right, but I protested all the same. He was talking about my parents, not those monsters I saw in the street attacking Daddy."

* * *

"Girl," he said quite forcefully now. "Your father sent for me to help him do a job. He is not here to help, so it has to be you and your friend. If she is able. We must…"

"I didn't let him finish," Patricia said. "I was with Daddy at the cemetery. I knew what needed to be done."

"This is my home," I told him. "You won't defile it."
"Then we must bring them outside, immediately."

"He was surprisingly strong for such a small man. He flung a blanket on the floor next to the bed, grabbed Daddy by the shoulders and hollered, "Well?"
"I took Daddy's ankles, and we lowered him to the blanket. Bernhard wrapped him as best he could, then we carried Daddy out behind the barn. Bernhard took hold of the blanket at Daddy's big shoulders. Carol and I took his feet. He was a gentleman, Bernhard was. He sent us to watch over Mother while he did what he had to. He said I didn't need to see what he was about to do, and he was right."
"I walked back to Mother's room, arm in arm with Carol. She tried her best to comfort me. Carol had been my friend long enough to know how dear Daddy was to me. Of course, I loved Mother, but Daddy was my beacon. Do you understand that, Roland?"
"I understand fully," he said. "With me, it was my Mom. My Dad was not a very giving man with his emotions. He was a good father, and a great provider for the family."
It was Roland's turn to take a moment. When he was ready he said, "Patricia, shall we go out to the porch?"
"I think that would be nice."

Chapter 37

Patricia only got halfway to the door before deciding a nap would do her better than a chat on the porch. Roland didn't need to be asked. He extended his arm to her. They padded over to the couch where he assisted her to her seat then retrieved a pillow and blanket. She curled up on the couch, and he tucked her in like he would a child in a crib.

"You're a sweet boy, Roland," she said, then closed her eyes.

Roland was in no mood to sit in front of his computer. He didn't want to go for a walk, and the heat from the sun squashed his desire to sit on the porch. He carried the lunch dishes to the kitchen, washed what needed washing and put whatever didn't get eaten back in the fridge. That finished, Roland began to wander through the old place.

He had seen most of the house, but across from Patricia's bedroom, a closed door held his attention. The door had been closed the whole time he had been there, and it called to him. It had to be her parents' room. He needed to see the room she had just described.

He made his way to the stairs leading to the second-floor hallway. Roland stood at the foot of the stairs, looking up to the dim cave-like corridor above. It must have been a truly grand staircase in its time, but too many decades of foot traffic had left it worn and shabby.

He placed a hand on the banister and marveled at the sturdiness of it. The wood, worn smooth from more than a century of hands gliding along its length, needed refinishing but was otherwise strong and sure.

Roland looked back over his shoulder to the closed door behind which his host slept. His conscience told him to stop. If Patricia wanted him to see that room, she would have invited him to have a look.

Curiosity, however, pushed him harder than his conscience held him back, and when his hand gripped the banister, his freedom of choice was taken from him. He had to go. He needed to go.

Roland placed his foot on the first step and slowly put pressure on that lead foot. He was waiting for the groan of the old wood to wake Patricia, and he would be caught. He feared she would see in him as nothing more than a snoopy reporter looking to spice up his story.

The stair gave no squawk, not even a mouse-like squeak. He tried the second with the same result, then the third. When he stood on the top step, Roland turned and listened for movement from the den where he left Patricia. The complete lack of sound in the house sent a shiver up his spine. His breathing seemed thunderous in the oppressive silence.

He padded over the faded carpet, his footfalls making a dull swish, thump. Standing in front of the door to the master bedroom, Roland could feel his heart trying to pound itself free of his chest. Nervous sweat trickled down his back.

He reached for the doorknob. It was a gaudy, ornate brass thing. The heat in the upstairs hall dried his throat, giving him an urge to cough.

When his hand made contact with the knob, he drew it back with a start. It felt like ice compared to the searing heat of the ambient air.

Taking a deep breath, exhaling slowly, he grabbed the knob, twisted it and pushed the door open. It swung freely, the hinges making no protest at being called into action.

Stepping into that room was like stepping back in time. The fabric of the drapes and bed covering were dull but sturdy looking. The paisley pattern on the bed complimented the floral wallpaper. The four-poster bed made of oak, or maybe cherry, sat unchanged since the spring of 1912, when it last gave rest to warm bodies.

This room was a shrine to Patricia's parents. The bed was made but other than that, it looked like she hadn't changed a thing in the one hundred years since it was last used. The only tell-tale sign that it hadn't been completely abandoned was the cleanliness. Not a speck of dust on any surface and the air, although hot, was not any more stale than the rest of the house.

Roland left the room. He pulled the door closed doing his best to be quiet. When the latch clicked into place, it occurred to him that the knob was no longer ice cold. He wondered, was it cold when he first grabbed it, or was it his mind playing tricks?

Satisfied that whatever evil that might have existed in this room had been taken out with the bodies of the Owens, Roland retreated.

When he stepped down from the last step to the ground floor, a clap of thunder erupted causing Roland to cry out. He felt his heart pounding in his chest and silently scolded himself for the childishness of his reaction.

"You were right again, Patricia," he whispered to himself. "The storm is here."

Chapter 38

Patricia found Roland sitting on the porch. He had nodded off, his chin rested on his chest without grace. His breathing had a rattled sound as he struggled to get air through his pinched airway. Sweat beaded on his cheeks.

Between garbled snores, he moaned and uttered unintelligible sounds. His left hand dangled at his side, his right curled in his lap, clenched in a fist and shaking.

He woke with a start when she placed her hand on his shoulder.

"You'll give yourself an awful stiff neck like that, Roland," she said.

He patted the hand that woke him, amazed at how cold it felt. "You might be right," he said, massaging his neck with his other hand. "Did you just wake up?"

"I've been up for a bit," she answered. "I fixed us a snack. Are you hungry?"

Roland followed her to the kitchen, where they ate in silence. He was still a bit bleary from his nap, but he suspected Patricia was trying to build up the courage to continue where she left off.

"I think you were dreaming when I woke you," she said.

"Really?"

"You were moaning, and trying to talk."

"I hope I didn't say anything embarrassing," he said with a smirk.

Patricia shook her head. "It was just some mumbling."

Roland didn't remember dreaming, but would not be surprised if he was plagued by nightmares when Patricia finished telling her story.

Without preamble, Patricia said, "I stayed."

"Sorry?"

"When Bernhard told me to go tend my mother. I stayed and watched him long enough to make sure he knew what he was doing. I couldn't leave Daddy to this man. Even if he claimed to be Daddy's friend, I had not heard of him before that day. So I stayed.

"He was carrying a small satchel, and he took a long knife from it. It happened so fast. He pulled back the blanket, exposing Daddy's head and neck. Daddy had time for a half scream, and Bernhard swiped that blade across his throat. Just like the boy, black gore surged from the wound. Bernhard drew the knife back through the gash, and Daddy's head detached from his neck. I must have made a noise. A gasp, or maybe I screamed, I don't know for sure.

Bernhard spun to look at me.

"I am sorry you had to see that, girl," he said. "It is the only way to give them peace."

"That was when I went back to the house with Carol. I turned and ran, Carol trying to keep up but she couldn't. I think I was at Mother's side before Carol managed to join me.

"He did the same to Mother. Afterward, we took them to the cemetery. The three of us dug those graves with no help from anyone.

"We don't have time for ceremony," Bernhard said. "It will be dark soon."

"He pushed Daddy into one hole, then Mother in the other. A body makes a dreadful sound when it falls into a hole like that. I know they could feel no pain, but I know I winced as though it were me falling down into the earth."

"I will give you a moment to say goodbye," Bernhard said.

"I walked away from him, and I knelt between the two open graves. I prayed that they would find peace, wherever they were. He was back as soon as I stood. He tossed a cup of kerosene in each hole and dropped a flaming piece of cloth.

"I will remember the sound always. *Whoosh*. Then billowing black smoke and angry orange flames spewed from the holes. The smell made me want to vomit, and the heat, I have never felt heat like that.

"We let the flames and smoke die out, then took to the shovels. There was nothing dignified about my parents' burial. It was fast, brutal, and without compassion.

"I didn't cry at the graveside. There was no time to grieve. We had a task to complete, and we had a deadly time limit. When I was alone, I cried myself to sleep. I have shed tears almost every day since. Tears for what was taken from me. Tears for the awfulness that was left behind."

Patricia's Journal—Wednesday, July 3, 1912

A man came today. He claims Daddy sent for him. Bernhard, Carol and I buried Mother and Daddy. I dare not close my eyes for fear I will relive the day.

I can't stop crying.

God, please take them into your house.

Patricia closed the book with shaky hands. She sat silent and motionless for a moment, then removed a tissue from her pocket and dabbed her eyes.

"Silly isn't it?" she said. "It's been one hundred years. After all these years I still cry for their loss."

Roland having led a more or less charmed life had little to offer with words, so he put his arm around her and sat in silence with her.

He felt her quiver and knew it was not cold that caused it. Patricia Owens needed to cry, and Roland would make sure she got whatever she needed from here on.

chapter 39

When Patricia finished shedding tears for her family, she rose from her seat without assistance and trod to the porch steps.

Roland looked after her without moving. He didn't know if she needed some separation to finish with her grieving or just wanted to stretch her legs, so he sat, waiting for his cue.

"Well," she said. "Are we going to walk, or are you going to sit there like an old man?"

He sprung to his feet, and in a second, Roland stood beside her, hand extended to assist her down the steps.

"By the time we finished with the interment of Mother and Daddy, it was getting dark. Bernhard rushed us onto our horses, and we rode like the wind. His horse was a ratty-looking nag, but that ugly horse could run like no other horse I have seen.

"Twice he had to pull up in order for us to catch him. If you believe what you see in the movies, I was just not a good rider, and that is why I couldn't keep up, but that wasn't it. I can tell you there was no one who could ride a horse better than I could when I was a girl. Others might say he had a superior horse. My horse was the fastest in the county. Daddy bought him from a thoroughbred farm in Kentucky. Can you imagine that? For all I know, my horse shared bloodlines with Man o' War. But for all that, he couldn't hold a candle to the ugly-looking animal that Bernhard rode.

"I could hear Carol calling from a hundred feet back to wait for her. We did, but Bernhard did so like a fawn in a wolf den, his gaze darting this way and that.

"It was full dark when we thundered up the main road. There wasn't a single person to be seen. No lights burned in the windows. The stained-glass windows at the church sparkled with color, but there was no joy in the sight of them. Not for me anyway.

"Carol's husband came running out to greet her. He just dropped the reins to the ground and pulled her into the church."

Patricia went into one of her trance-like stares, and Roland stood and shuffled his way along the edge of the road. He looked in the direction of the abandoned farm with the dead well.

Death lived in that well, and the strength within was growing. The ring of barren soil had doubled when he saw it last. He wondered how much more life had been consumed since then. How far could it go? Did the evil beneath that rock have the power to swallow the whole county? Could it get to the lake, and if it did, would it suck the life from the water, killing the fish and fowl that called Lake Huron home?

"You must promise to stay away from there, young man," Patricia re-iterated her earlier warning.

Roland spun at the sound of her voice. He didn't notice Patricia had rejoined him.

"It pulls at me," he said.

"I know all about that pull. I have battled it for a century. You have to be stronger than the pull." Patricia took his hand and squeezed it, emphasizing her point.

"I promise," he said.

"What happened after you got back to town?" Roland asked.

"Aunt Maggie was standing in the doorway to her house," she said, with a giggle. "She was so angry with me."

Roland's heart lightened a bit at the sound of her laugh. Each day that went by, Patricia had gotten months older. At least to Roland it looked that way. The giggle she let out while confessing her arrival had peeled away some of the years the last few days had etched into her.

"Bernhard rushed the horses into the stable behind the office, while I tried to calm Auntie down. We heard him slam and latch the door, then he came running around the building to meet us.

"I made a fuss when he tried to usher us inside. 'We have to put the horses away proper,' I told him."

"I bet he didn't have the horses' well-being set nearly as high as you, did he?" Roland asked.

That brought on a gale of laughter from the old woman. Roland looked on with some amusement as Patricia's face turned three shades of red. After all those years, she still went into hysterics at the thought of causing grief for poor Bernhard.

"You're right about that, Roland," she sputtered through her laughter. "He hurried us into Auntie's. The last thing I saw before Bernhard slammed the door was Carol's horse walking down the road, untethered."

"Did Carol get her horse back?" Roland asked.

"Oh, sure. It seems the creatures can feed on livestock, but they preferred not to." She was still giggling at the thought of that horse wandering around town all night without a worry in the world while the people cowered in their shelters.

Chapter 40

After Patricia regained control, she took his hand to lead him back toward the house. He accepted with grace.

"You are too kind, good lady," he said, tipping an imaginary hat.

She grinned, hooked her hand on his elbow, and they began the walk back.

"Tell me about Bernhard," Roland said.

"Well, it took some aggressive convincing to get Auntie to allow him beyond the small foyer. Not that she could have stopped him. He was a little man, but deceivingly strong and equally agile. He was inside before Auntie could put up too much fuss."

"She wouldn't have left him out in the street with all that was going on. Would she?" Roland said.

"As far as Auntie was concerned, Bernhard could have been one of those monsters."

"I guess he could have," he said. "But if he were, he could have killed you anywhere on the road."

"It's easy to say that now, but back then with all that was going on, we didn't trust family and friends, so this funny little stranger definitely got more than his share of sideways glances."

"I guess that is understandable," Roland said.

"When I explained to Auntie that Bernhard came to Kings Shore at Daddy's invitation, well then, Bernhard was given the best chair in Auntie's place. She ran into the kitchen, returning with a cup of tea and a jar of honey. When he was comfortable, he told us what he knew."

"Robert sent me a wire," Bernhard began. "He told me what he found the night he returned to this hell town."

"Kings Shore is no hell town," Aunt Maggie said. "It was heaven on earth, until a few weeks ago."

"An apple can be heavenly on your tongue," Bernhard said. "But if you wait too long to eat it, it goes bad. That is what has happened here. The apple has gone bad."

"If you feel that way, then why come all this way, at risk of life and limb?" Aunt Maggie said.

"Robert Owens was a good friend. He would have done no less for me. When his message arrived requesting my help, I came immediately."

"Now that you are here, what will you do?" Auntie said.

"I will wait for the sun to rise, and go back the way I came, and I suggest you ride out with me."

Patricia stopped walking and looked up at Roland. "That was when I joined the conversation. Auntie was struck dumb. We both looked on Bernhard like the cavalry had arrived, and this runt of a man announces that as soon as he can, he is going to turn tail and run." Patricia's volume rose with an ire that remained vibrant through the ages.

"You can't just leave, there are people here who need help," I told him.

"Madame," he said. "I came to help my friend. I helped his child to bury him and his wife. Unless you wish to join your mother and father," he said staring right at me. "You are well advised to go."

"This is our home," I told him. "Like my father, I am not afraid to die protecting it."

"Miss," he said in a tone that was barely more than a whisper. "There are much worse things than death in this town. I think you know that."

* * *

"I had to agree with him on that, Roland."

"But you still refused to leave," Roland said.

"Yes," she agreed. "And God bless him, Bernhard stayed too. I don't think he really planned on leaving in the morning. He just needed to know that we were going to be with him every step."

chapter 41

Taking a seat on a bench, Patricia took her journal from Roland's left hand and opened it to the page marked by the ribbon.

"At night, we need only stay inside. They will not come in," Bernhard began.

"They are very strong," I told him. "What is to stop them from breaking down the door, or crashing through a window?"

"I don't know the answer to that, I only know they won't. Maybe they have a fear of enclosure, but I don't think that is it. We found your parents in their home."

"Auntie made a choking sound when she heard that. Poor dear. We had to pause, Bernhard's explanation to Auntie about the burial," Patricia told Roland, "was dreadfully shocking to her."

"It seems," Bernhard continued, "that they will enter a structure they feel safe in, but they will not force entry to just any building. No matter how hungry they are."

"What's to stop them from tossing a torch on the roof and forcing us into the street?" Auntie asked.

"Fire," I said. "They catch fire like they have been soaked in kerosene."

"That's right, Miss," Bernhard said. "Only two things will set terror in their eyes, fire and the glorious rays of the sun."

"But they can be killed," I insisted.

"Yes, Miss. But they do not fear death. They are already dead."

Patricia and Roland had turned into the yard. Roland's Bimmer sparkled in the afternoon sun. The air was warm, with a breeze that was just enough to make the day perfect for a walk in the air. A breeze came from the lake and carried with it a sweet aroma.

"That was when we heard Minnie Simmons. Pete Simmons, a trapper, kept a house in town. We heard Minnie holler at him to hurry in the house. We looked out to see Pete shuffling down the middle of the road. We knew he was one of them. I yelled at Minnie to get inside, but she didn't listen. Maybe she didn't hear me over her own calls for Pete.

"Minnie ran out to greet him," Patricia paused. "He put his arms around her like he had done a thousand times. But this time he pulled her in close and with a savagery I didn't think possible, tore the side of her neck open with his teeth.

"Minnie made a slight humph sound, and then we could only hear the sucking and slurping as Pete drank from her. Another one of those things came, and Pete just dropped Minnie in the street and disappeared. The other one knelt next to Minnie and finished her.

"When he couldn't draw another drop from her dry carcass, he stood and looked right at us. It was like he sensed our eyes watching him. One moment he was standing over Minnie's corpse, the next he stood on the walk right in front of Auntie's door.

"I didn't even see Bernhard leave the room, but all of a sudden he was standing in front of the door with a bottle. It looked like a wine bottle with a length of rag dangling from it. In his other hand, he held a burning candle.

"He motioned to the door with his eyes. Auntie just stood with her hands over her mouth. I shook my head, the last thing I wanted was to open the door and let that thing inside. Bernhard made another gesture to the door, but this time his eyes burned with anger. For a second I feared him more than the monsters outside, and I pulled the door open. He touched the flame of the candle to the cloth and tossed it at the thing before the door was completely open. The bottle crashed at the demon's feet, and the kerosene from the bottle set the thing ablaze."

Patricia stopped again, placing her hands to her ears. Trying to block out a noise only she could hear. Roland placed his hand on her elbow and steadied her as they climbed the steps to the front door.

"The scream," she said. "I swear it could be heard for miles. Ear-splitting pitch and volume that not even today's technology could match.

"It walked down the middle of the street. After the initial shock, the screaming stopped. A human-shaped torch, taking an evening stroll. Then it fell, face first to the ground. Black, acrid smoke filled the air.

"The cool air didn't move enough to make a candle flame flicker that night. The dreadful smoke hung in the air like a toxic cloud. The fear of what was out there saved many of us choking from the stink of it. We all had our windows closed that night.

"Several more monsters rushed into the street. Drawn to the screams like moths to a flame. They stood around the burning abomination, not close enough to put themselves in any danger but they encircled it. When the flames burned out, they turned away from the macabre sight and stared at the buildings lining the street.

"It was ominous. Everyone in town got the feeling that at least one of those things was staring accusingly at them. I was included in that. They have some kind of telepathy, and I felt fear growing stronger inside of me. I swear I felt my own heart pounding in my chest before they broke their gaze."

"What about Bernhard?" Roland asked. "Did he feel it?"

"Maybe more than the rest," she replied. "He did set their friend afire."

"Friend?" Through a slight chuckle, Roland's voice sounded doubtful.

Chapter 42

Maybe we can defeat them. With Bernhard's help maybe we can survive this plague.

With Bernhard's help just maybe Mother and Daddy can be avenged.

God, thank you for bringing Bernhard to us.

Patricia read this entry, then stood and left the room, leaving the journal on the coffee table. Roland watched the old woman shuffle through the door at the far side of the room, the smooth glide of her gait on the day they met no longer in evidence.

Sitting alone in her study, Roland looked at the page in front of him. Maybe we can defeat them. He tried to imagine the frail, small woman he now knew, at twenty, battling supernatural bloodthirsty demons.

He couldn't. Roland Millhouse opened his laptop. He inserted the earbuds into his mini recorder and pushed Play. As Patricia's words filled his head, Roland began to type.

The church bell rang just after sunrise. Bernhard pulled the rope rhythmically while Patricia stood on the church steps waiting. An abomination about three hundred yards away still smoldered where the thing had fallen last night. All that remained in the spot where it fell was a blackened stain of scorched earth.

Jacob Hebert was the first to respond to the church bell. A stout man in his early forties, dressed in overalls and a straw hat, Jacob greeted Patricia with his usual verve.

Jacob grew up with Patricia's father, and she had known him her whole life. Like all the inhabitants of Kings Shore in the summer of 1912, he looked much older than his years, in spite of a smile that started at his lips and went all the way to his eyes.

"What has happened, Little Miss?" Jacob called when he was within shouting distance. Patricia was slightly taller than Jacob, but he had called her Little Miss from the time she was born, and to him, she would always be Little Miss.

"There is a man here to help us," Patricia called to Jacob. "He has come from afar, and he knows how to fight them."

"Who is this man?" Jacob asked.

"I will introduce him when everyone has arrived," she told him. "But I will tell you this, Daddy sent for him." The women of Kings Shore of 1912 didn't put off a man's questions, but Patricia Owens was almost royalty. When the Owens spoke, the people of Kings Shore listened.

"What can I do?" Jacob asked.

"Direct everyone into the church. We will begin in thirty minutes," the young woman said.

With Jacob there to direct all comers into the church, Patricia opened the door and entered the building. She left the door wide open. Sunshine and fresh morning air filled the room and the gloom of the previous night retreated to the shadows beneath the pews and in the corners and behind the altar. The bell gonged repeatedly, vibrating the stained glass windows. The bell's chime was smooth and the tone clear, but the volume was deafening.

The pews filled in much less time than would normally be the case. Most of the inhabitants of the surrounding farms had stopped sleeping in their homes. They worked the farms in the day, then bunked with family or friends in town. Safety in numbers was the mantra of the day.

At just after 7:00 a.m., Patricia strode to the pulpit, and the din of nervous chatter dulled, then stopped completely.

"All are here that's coming," Jacob called from the front pew. "Why have you called us here, Little Miss?"

"Before Daddy," she paused there, a knot trying to rise in her throat. "When my father heard of the goings on here, he sent word to his friend, Bernhard Werner. Mr. Werner has come to Kings Shore, and he knows how to fight the… those demons of the night."

"Why should we put our faith in a complete stranger?" a man's voice called from the back.

"How many of you saw that smoldering foulness in the street on your way here this morning?" Patricia answered.

More than half the people in the church raised a hand. Some hands shot up straight and high, while some of the more tentative citizens held their hands at shoulder height and looked around to see who was with them. A brief moment of chatter filled the church with a buzz.

"That was one of the demons," Patricia said. "Mr. Werner killed it single-handed."

A murmur of hushed voices hummed through the room. Heads turned from side to side as the people of Kings Shore discussed the news they just heard. Some pointed up to the front of the room. Heads nodded and shook as they all discussed the idea of entrusting their safety to a man they had never laid eyes on until walking into the church that morning.

"Killin' one of them don't mean this man knows shit about shit," an irritated man hollered from somewhere in back. "There could be a hundred of those demons out there in the woods."

This brought another wave of discussion, only this time the volume rose as the talk turned heated between some of the more frightened folk. Humans, like any animal that's cornered and scared, will more times than not act out with aggression.

Bernhard took the Bible from the pulpit. It was one of those monstrosities the preachers use, and he dropped it on the floor. That book made a bang so loud you would have thought he fired a scattergun in there.

* * *

Roland paused the audio. He couldn't help but grin at the sound of Patricia's laugh while she told this. It was obvious to him that she grew very fond of Bernhard during the short time they had been together.

Roland pushed the Play button to continue.

The crash of that book on the floorboards brought a hush to the room in a heartbeat.

Some of the men even raised their rifles at the front, ready to shoot anything that moved. It was quite tense for a few moments.

When the church went quiet, Bernhard picked up the good book, put it back on the altar, and you would swear that little man grinned.

"He sounds like he was quite a character," Roland remembered telling her.

"Oh, he was that alright," she said, laughing again.

"Here is what I know," Bernhard began. "The demons are not immortal. As you have all seen by now, they can be killed. They have weaknesses."

"They don't look so weak to me," the same man who called out earlier said.

"They are most definitely not weak," Bernhard replied in his calm, almost bored tone. "But they do have weaknesses. For instance, fire is one, as Miss Owens will attest. If you can touch them with a flame, they ignite as though they have kerosene in their veins."

"That's the truth," Curtis Davidson called out. "They came to my place. My boy was among 'em. Killed his own mother. I found the lot in my barn the next morning. Burned it to the ground with the demons inside. I have never seen fire burn so hot. As terrible as it must have been for them in there, they would not come out into the sun. Screams like that can only come from Satan himself." Curtis sat in the pew next to his youngest, buried his face in his hands and wept.

As it turns out, the voice from the back was Alfred Sharpe, and by this time, he had made his way to the front of the church.

"So that's it then," Alfred said. "We just torch 'em when they come into town, and the ones that don't burn will move on."

"It will not be as easy as that," Bernhard told him. "They will not stand still while you set them ablaze. These things move faster than anything you have seen before. At a full run, your eyes can barely see them. It is like trying to watch the wings of a hummingbird. If they see you with fire, they will evade your attack, and before you know where they went, they will be seizing you from the rear and your life will be ended."

"Then that information is of little value, Mr. Werner," Alfred said.

"Alone, I would have to agree. As I said, they have weaknesses. These creatures cannot live in sunlight, so if it is possible to find their resting place in the daytime, they are defenseless. You can drag them into the sun, and the things will perish in the most heinous fashion imaginable. Also, they cannot survive for long without their head."

"What do you mean, for long?" Alfred asked. This brought another round of murmuring. Bernhard stood silent until he had everyone's attention.

"If you remove the head of one of those demons, you must cast it far away from the body. Then while it is defenseless, set the carcass ablaze. They can reattach any body part if they get hold of it within a few minutes. Even their heads."

"Is that all then?" Alfred looked dejected. "It seems the only way to kill them is to get so close that we are at more risk of death than the monsters."

"You speak true, sir," Bernhard replied. "Many of you will be dead when the final chapter here is written. Some of you will most likely become one of them."

An eruption of dissent filled the church, as scared and angry townsfolk faced a bleak and uncertain future. Bernhard turned his back on the crowd and walked to the reverend's chair against the back wall of the pulpit.

These people had two choices. They could set out at sunrise, riding as far and fast as they could and with some luck, get far enough away before dusk to be safe. Those who chose to stay could fight, try to find a safe hiding place every night, or die. Bernhard would sit and wait for them to come up with this conclusion on their own. That was the only way they would see it for the truth.

Chapter 43

Roland woke to the creaking sound of Patricia's rocking chair on the hardwood floor in her parlor. Once again, he had fallen asleep on her old couch. Once again, she had covered him with an old afghan, and once more he ached all over for the experience.

Before he joined his host, Roland sauntered across the room to the kitchen door. He couldn't help but grin. Patricia had a tray set up on the counter, complete with sliced fruitcake and a crystal pitcher of what turned out to be cranberry juice.

"You're a good boy, Roland Millhouse," Patricia said when he carried the tray into the room. "I think I will be sad to see you go."

"Are you getting ready to send me on my way?"

"Not ever," she said. "Don't even think it. But you will not want to spend too much more time in the company of an ancient relic like me."

He poured two glasses of juice, placed a slice of cake on each plate and set one of each on the table in front of her.

"I could hear you clicking away on that machine a while ago," she said. "Do you think anyone will be interested in the ramblings of an old woman?"

"It is really hard to say what will interest today's readers, Patricia. If a celebrity writes a book, millions will line up to buy it. A teen idol can write a memoir and sell millions. How can anyone who hasn't lived to see twenty years have enough life experience to write a memoir? Yet they do it, and it sells. Will they line up to buy a story of vampires attacking a village one hundred years ago? Probably not. Does your story need to be told? Absolutely."

"Where did I leave off?" she asked.

"Bernhard was trying to explain the weaknesses of the vampires," Roland said.

Patricia giggled, nibbled on her cake, then sipped some juice. She dabbed at the corners of her mouth with a napkin with such grace Roland would have been easily convinced she came from royalty.

"Bernhard wasn't much for sugar coating the facts," she said. "It took the people in that church a long time to quiet down after hearing their chances of survival were not terribly good. These were just simple farmers and loggers. They were not trained soldiers. Even after all the tragedy that had befallen Kings Shore to that point, they still did not want to believe their own fate could be walking such a fine line."

When they finally hushed, Jacob Hebert said, "What is your plan? You do have a plan do you not?"

Bernhard stood and stepped back to the pulpit. A few hushed conversations continued, and that little man just stood there until every person in that room had stopped talking. Bernhard insisted on two things. When he spoke, he would have everyone's complete attention, and if someone interrupted him while he spoke, he would stop talking. Bernhard would stare down at any man who spoke while he was speaking. He cared not one iota how big they were. Bernhard didn't fear the vampires, and he sure as hell feared no mortal man.

"During the day," Bernhard continued, "we will search for the creatures' hiding places. If you find one, drag it into the sun. But be careful; they are helpless, but even a hare will struggle in the talons of an owl to preserve itself. It must be full sun. No shadows, no clouds."

"What do we do at night?" Jacob asked.

"Stay inside," Bernhard said. "This is most important. They can go into buildings, but they won't. Nobody knows why this is so, but please believe it."

It was Alfred's turn to speak. "So all we do is stay inside at night, and hunt them down after sunrise?"

"That is the simple explanation," Bernhard said. "Unfortunately it will not be as easy as that. Those things have a way of coaxing people from their homes. They make no sound, but somehow their call can be as loud as a mermaid's song."

"You mean they can hypnotize people?" Donna Mason said.

"I don't know if that is what they do, Miss…"

"Mason," she said. "Donna Mason."

"Well, Miss Mason, it is best if nobody stays alone. They have a way of sensing that. Like a pride of lions stalking a zebra that has strayed from the herd. Any person alone after sunset is at a higher risk of being lured outside by the monsters. They can talk. They even remember their existence before they turned, but most choose not to use verbal language."

"Why not?" Donna asked.

"I don't know," Bernhard replied.

"Seems to me," Alfred said, "that there is more you don't know than what you do."

"You have a knack of seeing through to the truth, sir," Bernhard said, looking directly at him.

"Why not tell us what you do know," Alfred jibed.

"I know if they come upon a former loved one, and make no mistake, they are former loved ones. These things do not bring family loyalties with them when they turn. But they will use it if they can. They may try to deceive you into thinking they are not demons. They have been known to rejoice when reuniting with family. Before you know it, you are in their arms, and when that happens, it will be the end for you."

Curtis had stopped weeping. He didn't speak this time, just sat nodding as Bernhard explained the behavior he had witnessed from his own son. The behavior that caused his wife to be taken by that son.

"Mr. Werner," Donna said. "This has all been quite informative, but is there a plan?"

* * *

Patricia sipped her juice, then looked to Roland. "Roland, my old bones are seizing up like an un-oiled machine. What do you say we take a walk?"

Roland downed his juice and sprung to his feet. "That is a great idea." He extended his hand in what had become their ritual, and she gratefully took it.

Chapter 44

They walked in silence until they got to the end of the driveway. The sun was high in the sky. A few wispy clouds hovered in an otherwise brilliant expanse of blue. The humidity had left the area taking with it the stagnant, oppressive heat. In its place was mild air made more comfortable by an intermittent breeze.

"Did he have a plan?" Roland finally asked.

"Bernhard?" She chuckled. "Bernhard wasn't much on planning. He was big on acting. Jacob Hebert was the planner, and boy did he. By the end of the day, he made sure that at least two people stayed in every home. He organized a meeting to discuss where the vampires might be hiding during the day. He had all the women making up firebombs like the one Bernhard used to burn the monster in front of Auntie's."

"It sounds like Jacob and Bernhard made the perfect pair," Roland said.

"They may well have, but Jacob didn't live long enough to test that theory out."

"What happened?"

"Poor Jacob," she said. "It was just after sunset. It wasn't quite dark yet. Jacob had this ratty old dog. His name was Winston. From his window, Jacob saw Winston eyeing something across the street. He opened the door and called to Winston, but the dog wouldn't come. He never was the brightest dog, but Jacob loved him like some people love a child. Do you know what I mean, Roland?"

Roland nodded with a grin.

"Anyway, it was like I said. Just after sunset, but not quite dark yet so Jacob thought it would be fine to go out and drag Winston into the house. I heard him holler at Winston to come.

"I went to the window. Bernhard heard him too. He swung that door open and yelled for Jacob to get back inside."

"He didn't make it," Roland said when Patricia paused.

"No, Roland. He heard Bernhard's warning, but before he could react a demon that once was a kindly man named John Moore appeared in front of Jacob. It was awful to watch. Poor Jacob smiled at the thing, not realizing that it only looked like John Moore.

"It snatched Jacob by the hair so fast I can't remember seeing it move. Jacob's scream was so high, he sounded almost like a girl. Then John Moore's new fangs sank deep into Jacob's throat. Winston latched onto the demon, but it took no notice. It didn't even try to dislodge that dog from its arm.

"Jacob fought the thing for a few seconds, then his arms fell to his side and he stood there like he was sound asleep standing up. It looked like a lover's embrace until I saw Jacob's blood dripping onto the road. Even in the fading light, his blood glowed bright crimson.

"I screamed at it, Roland. 'You leave him alone,' I yelled. Well, that monster released his grip on Jacob and looked right at me. His mouth opened into a bloody grin."

Patricia stopped walking. Her hands came to her face as though she were watching the horrific scene all over again. Roland put his arm around her shoulders and waited for her to continue.

"So long ago, and I can still see poor Jacob swaying in place beside that monster. Bernhard grew furious. I still don't know if his anger was aimed at Jacob for letting himself be caught like that, at the vampire, or at himself for not being able to stop what was happening.

"Bernhard turned and ran from the room. When he got back, he had one of those damnable firebombs. The vampire had returned to feeding from Jacob by the time Bernhard sprung from the front door. He set the cloth wick of that bottle afire so fast I thought maybe he had a touch of supernatural in him.

"The flame got that thing's attention, and this time it wasn't grinning. It hissed like a cat, grabbed poor dear Jacob by the hair and twisted his head right off his neck. The sound of that still wakes me in the night. Jacob's body fell to the ground in a heap. I could see blood squirt from the stump where Jacob's head had just been. The poor dear, after he was de-capitated his heart continued to beat a few times. The dreadful creature stood with Jacob's head dangling from his hand for a moment. He had a look of satisfaction. Like he was telling us that Jacob's fate had been set in motion by our interference. Then he threw the head at Bernhard.

"Bernhard was able to dodge the macabre thing. It sailed right into the house through the open door and crashed into the wall with a sicken-ing thud. I am sorry to say that I screamed like a frightened child.

"His face. When Jacob's head fell to the floor, his eyes were wide open and looking at me. At least it seemed that way to me at the time. A small pool of blood gathered on the floor around it. It was a dreadful thing to see."

Patricia resumed walking, and Roland took his place at her side. He offered his arm, but she declined. Her steps were small and shaky at first, but as she continued toward the cemetery, her gait steadied a bit.

"The vampire disappeared before Bernhard could toss the bottle. De-jected, Bernhard pulled that burning cloth from the bottle and tossed it to the ground, getting a nasty burn to his fingers for the effort.

"It looked like magic. Do you know what I mean? The way they ap-peared and disappeared was like something from a movie. It wasn't really. The damn things were just so fast that you couldn't see them move. Can you believe that, Roland?"

"Patricia," he replied, "a few days ago I would have said you were as crazy as this whole thing sounds. Now, if you told me the earth was flat and Bigfoot lived in a room in your attic, I would believe it."

"Well, I doubt that is true, Roland. That you would believe those things, I mean. Anyway, everyone in this area knows that Bigfoot lives in the barn out back of my house."

They both had a welcome laugh at that. It was a rest from the hideous tale, and Roland and Patricia reveled in it.

"What does he eat?" Roland asked.

"Reporters," she said through continued giggles.

"So all those snacks and glasses of lemonade were just meant to fatten me up for the beast?"

Patricia shrugged and continued walking.

Chapter 45

Patricia took advantage of every one of the benches the good citizens of Kings Shore placed along the road between her house and the graveyard.

The first time Roland walked along with her, she had no trouble getting to the old bench she herself had placed at the cemetery gate. Roland looked at her now and wondered if she would have to sit here alone while he went back for the car. She looked better than yesterday, but she didn't look good.

Her shoulders slumped, and her hands had the slightest tremor. The confident, graceful strides she took on that first walk had been replaced by timid, shaky shuffling. She wasn't quite ready for the aid of a walker, but if she continued to slide at this rate, she would need something before the end of the week.

"Will you be okay to get back? You seem a bit fatigued," Roland said.

"I just need to rest, don't you fret about me at all."

"While you rest, I think I will have another look at the gravestones," Roland said.

"Jacob is two rows behind Mother and Daddy," she said. "Just off to the right a bit."

After one hundred years of visiting this place, Roland had little doubt that Patricia could map out the entire place while sitting at her kitchen table.

The marker at Jacob Hebert's grave was unassuming. He lay beneath a small grey granite stone inscribed with his name, the date of birth and death. No epitaph, no message celebrating a life complemented the dates. No carved decorations or crosses on the stone.

Roland stared down at the name, Jacob Hebert. The way Jacob met his end played like a movie inside Roland's head. It was like he was envisioning what Patricia had told him. He was certain something or someone projected the images into his mind from some unseen transmitter.

Roland cried out and began to shake as he saw the monster rip the head from Jacob's body. He staggered back from the grave, tripping over a small headstone and falling back.

Sitting in the grass, Roland squeezed his eyes closed so tight it hurt. The images didn't fade. It was as though he were floating over the headless body of Jacob Hebert. He watched in horror as the poor man's head sailed through the open door. He could hear the young voice of Patricia Owens, screaming in the distance.

Roland pushed himself away from Jacob's headstone until he crashed into another granite marker. Without reading the name on this one, he sprang to his feet, still hearing the screams. The images were gone, but he still heard the terrified wailing from the past.

Like a sprinter, Roland thrust himself forward, wanting nothing more in life than to be free of the carnage. As if the cemetery wanted him to stay, the grass beneath his feet tore away from the earth, and Roland fell to his knees.

A second effort had him tripping on an exposed tree root, and he went down again. Roland Millhouse crawled over the graves of at least five victims of the summer of 1912 before he tried to gain his feet again. His heart was pounding, sweat ran into his eyes, and his breathing came in enormous gulps. His left hand bled from an injury he didn't remember getting. When he got back to the gate, Patricia stood and began to walk back in the direction of home. She didn't speak, and Roland was glad for it. He wasn't sure he was capable of talking.

Chapter 46

"In the morning they took Jacob's remains to the cemetery. No coffin, no marker, just a hastily dug hole. They placed him in, poured kerosene on him and set him ablaze."

Patricia, seated on a bench at the side of the road, shook her head, still trying to make peace with the indignity of it.

"When the flames went out, a couple of loggers went back to the grave and filled it in. No preacher said any words. Other than Winston, Jacob had no family in Kings Shore."

"What became of that dog?" Roland asked.

"Wouldn't you know it," she said. "That dog went mad. Some thought it was due to the loss of Jacob. I knew that wasn't the case. He bit down on that vampire the whole time it was feeding on Jacob. Poor thing had to get some of that monster's blood in his mouth. Whatever makes those things what they are is in the blood. Old Winston swallowed enough of it to turn him mad, no doubt about that."

"Did he get sick and die?" Roland asked.

"Bernhard shot him. In the morning, Winston was pulling big chunks of flesh from Jacob's body. When Bernhard saw that dog eating his own master, he was appalled. Of course, we all were, but it was Bernhard who acted. He retrieved his rifle and shot Winston five times.

"You know, Roland. I think Bernhard really took a liking to Jacob. Bernhard wasn't a man who had friends, but if anyone in Kings Shore was apt to become friends with Bernhard Werner, it would have been Jacob."

"From the sound of it, they complimented each other. Yin and yang sort of stuff," Roland said.

Patricia didn't reply to that. She gave a short nod and plodded on toward home.

Chapter 47

Patricia's Journal—Sunday, July 7, 1912
   Every able-bodied person in town searched for the demons' hiding places. Where could they be? Daddy, I need you. Earl and Claudia Desmond went missing. I hope they escaped this place.

Patricia closed her journal. Roland reached over the coffee table in her parlor and took the book. He placed it on the table and waited.

"They didn't escape," she said, breaking the silence. "Earl and Claudia I mean."

"Did they return in the night?"

"That is a delicate way of putting it, Roland. Yes, they came back the next night. They walked into town like a couple of drunks. I don't know if it was because they were just new, but my thought is the demon blood was getting weaker. I think the farther down the family tree they got from the original monster, the weaker the resulting offspring."

"Sounds about right," Roland said.

"When I mentioned it to Bernhard, he went into deep thought. He didn't speak for the rest of the night. When he finally did speak, it was a revelation."

"People," Bernhard said. "I think we need to find the original monster.

The one that brought this plague on your community. We need to search every home and outbuilding until we find it."

"That could take months," Peter Malcolm said.

"Then we had better get started," Bernhard shot back.

Patricia giggled a bit. There was little in her story that would bring an urge for laughs of any kind, but when she spoke of Bernhard's character traits, it always brought an endearing glow to her face. "That Bernhard, he didn't take complaining in stride. It was a waste of breath in his mind," she assured him.

Roland marveled at the look of admiration that came over her when she spoke of Bernhard. The same expression she had when she spoke of her father. That is how it appeared to Roland.

"We split into four groups. Auntie, Bernhard and I went south, toward my home. We stopped at every farm and home along the east side of the road.

"It was near dusk when we got to this house. Bernhard ran through the outbuildings, while I went inside with Auntie. That whole day we searched for them. We found nothing.

"I was so tired and felt defeated. An entire day spent scouring the area, only to settle into this house knowing that those things would be out there hunting our friends and neighbors."

"It was your first day," Roland said. "It would have been quite a miracle to find them on the first day."

"I know that now, but back then I felt so low. The only thing that helped to pick my spirits up at all was being back home. In spite of what Bernhard and I had been through here, it was home."

"It's always good to get back home," Roland agreed.

"I slept in my own room that night. Auntie slept in the guest room that Daddy had set up just for her. Bernhard didn't sleep much, if at all. He stayed down here with a dozen of those bottle bombs and his rifle. Mother's room remained closed. I could not bear to look in there. Auntie or Bernhard must have gone in there sometime to replace the bedding. It was weeks before I grew brave enough to enter that room to find it the way it is today."

With that, Patricia excused herself from the room and Roland let himself out.

Chapter 48

Patricia gave a wave and a smile as Roland arrived. Seated on the porch swing, she looked comfortable in her dowdy sweater and wool slacks. The air had cooled overnight, and a mostly cloudy sky prevented the sun from warming the air.

Roland no longer looked the part of reporter on the rise, dressed in jeans and a long-sleeved blue polo. The gloomy morning and fine layer of dust left the Bimmer looking equally morose.

"I brought breakfast," he said, holding up a Tim Horton's bag. "Can I tempt you with tea and a bagel?"

"You most certainly can," she assured him.

They spoke of mundane things while they ate. The weather, a local art show, and even the coming blueberry festival filled the conversation. When Patricia had sipped the last of her tea, she opened her journal and read.

Patricia's Journal—Monday, July 8, 1912

We searched and searched. Will we ever find them? If we do, will we be able to do what we need to do? I trust Mr. Werner with my life, but there is a feeling of dread in this place. Daddy, I have never needed you more than now.

"I was feeling quite down the night I wrote that. I remember sitting on my own bed, thinking that the end was coming, but not the end we all hoped for," Patricia said.

"I bet the whole town felt the same way," Roland replied.

"Many in the town were of no use. They scurried about during the day and hid in their basements at night. The Gignacs were found in their beds. Pierre shot his wife and kids, then put the barrel of the gun in his mouth and pulled the trigger. He left a note."

"He decided it was better to go like that than be taken by the vampires?" Roland asked.

With a nod, she said, "I can't blame him, but I was like Daddy. If I was going to go down, I would go down fighting.

"I think many of the folk in Kings Shore thought the Gignacs' way out of town might be the best way. There was no quit in Bernhard though. During breakfast, he pushed me and Auntie for ideas on where the vampires could be hiding. We both mentioned every abandoned cabin and farm we knew of within a day's ride in every direction.

"Bernhard had me draw him a map of them all. He went away for an hour or two, and came back with a plan."

"A plan for the day's hunt?" Roland asked.

Patricia just nodded.

"As it turned out, it was a pretty good plan. By noon, we found them, some of them at least, in a barn about three miles south of here. It looked normal enough. The grey wood structure leaned something awful. I was terrified to go inside. Not because I thought there might be vampires in there, but because I thought it could fall down on our heads."

Roland snickered for a moment, while Patricia giggled. Her jocular mood faded when she resumed her tale.

"When we opened the door and looked inside, we thought it was another wasted effort. It was just an empty barn, filled with molding hay. We were about to leave when a rat scurried out from the hayloft. That rodent trundled right over our feet. That in itself would not normally be something to catch your attention, but when two more came rushing out from the same spot, Bernhard decided to take a closer look. I followed with Auntie right behind me.

"The air in there had a stale foulness. I could see the anxiety in Bernhard's eyes when he looked back to check on us. Auntie looked as frightened as I felt.

"Bernhard kicked some old hay aside and uncovered a hand. It must have sensed we were there because the hand disappeared under the hay. The whole pile shifted. It sounded like a hundred rats were moving around under there."

"Vampires," Roland said.

She nodded. "Vampires."

"Bernhard found an old pitchfork in the back of the barn, and he jabbed it in the hay. At first, he found nothing. He started to dig. Hay flew everywhere as he frantically burrowed deeper in. The smell of dust and mold filled our noses. I could hear Bernhard's breathing. He dug so vigorously that I feared he would faint from exhaustion.

"He stopped suddenly and looked to me, then to Auntie. A devilish grin spread over his face. Bernhard probed with the fork, gently moving the last of the hay from a man's face."

"Did you recognize him?" Roland asked.

"It was John Moore," she said. "I looked down at him with hatred for what he did to Jacob. Years later, I grew to hate myself for that. John Moore was a nice man. The demon that killed Jacob was but a hollow image of the man it resembled. No more than a walking photograph."

"What did Bernhard do next?" Roland feared hearing the details. He didn't know if he could stand to view any more of Patricia's stories in his head, but he was powerless against his desire to hear more.

"He ordered us from the barn. There was no mistaking his tone, and we did not argue. Auntie and I fled with great haste into the bright sun of the late morning.

"I was never so glad to stand in the sunlight as I was that morning, Roland.

"Bernhard followed a moment later, walking with a leisure that might be considered odd given the circumstance.

"Seconds after he walked to our side, white smoke whooshed from the barn door."

"He set the barn on fire?" Roland asked.

"It wasn't long after we saw the smoke, we heard the first scream.

The sound was horrific to a degree that words cannot explain. We covered our ears, but it did no good. I was certain my ears would bleed from the cries of the agonized demons within the fire."

As she had before, Patricia covered her ears with her hands as if to block the sounds she heard a century ago. As he had done before, Roland placed his hand on her shoulder in hopes of giving her comfort. Patricia took her hand from her ear and placed it over his.

"Four," she said. "We counted four separate voices coming from the inferno. Only one dared leave the shelter of the barn. Bright blue flames came running toward us. Me and Auntie shuffled back as fast as our legs would carry us, but not Bernhard. He stood defiant, as though he wanted that thing to come to him."

Patricia stood, shaking her head the way people do when they look on somebody doing something amazing. When you can't believe what you are seeing and you're in complete awe of what a mere human is doing.

"As soon as that thing ran out of the shadow of the barn into the bright sunshine, it stopped running. You wouldn't think anything could cause more pain than being burned alive. When the sun fell upon that vampire, her screams turned to something I can only describe as a life-time of pain and terror all molded into one moment."

"She?" Roland said.

"We could make out the remnants of a dress that the flames hadn't yet consumed when she left the barn," Patricia said. "The fabric didn't last long. When the sun hit her, it was like fanning the flames. The fire went from blue to white. It hurt my eyes to look at it. Something so brilliant, yet the smoke it gave off was black and acrid. Like the flame was a cleansing agent and the smoke the filth being washed away."

"Patricia," Roland said. "The way you tell a story, it is truly a shame you didn't write this down. You can be as elegant as any poet of the ages."

"Isn't that why you stayed?" she said. "To write the story and make it a best seller."

Roland flushed a bit and shrugged. "It would surely be more impres-sive with your words."

Chapter 49

Roland Millhouse screamed himself awake. He squinted at the bright red numbers on the digital clock next to his bed.

It was 3:33 a.m.

His chest heaved, and perspiration soaked his face. The sheets clung to his damp, naked body. Roland could feel his heart hammering, and he swore he could actually hear it beat.

"Jesus," he whispered.

Patricia's telling of the fire at the barn was clear. She left no room to doubt the terror of the moment. Now, having just relived the awful scene in his dreams, Roland was beginning to understand just how much of a toll this story had placed on Patricia Owens.

He resigned himself to not getting another good night sleep until this ordeal was finished. Until Patricia's story was told and written, he would have to learn to exist on less sleep. Even after he moved on, Roland didn't think he would ever enjoy another peaceful night's sleep.

Knowing he would not get back to sleep this night, Roland dressed and walked to the Tim Hortons. With a coffee in one hand and his laptop case in the other, he walked to the table furthest from the counter. With his back to the corner, he removed his computer from the case and started it up.

"There's no Wi-Fi in here, dude," a voice called from the counter.

Roland looked up to see Colin, the pimple-faced kid who sold him the coffee, looking at him.

"Sorry?" Roland said.

"Wi-Fi," he said again. "There's no Wi-Fi in here."

"No problem," Roland replied. "Just going to check some notes anyway."

When his desktop appeared, Roland opened a document titled, Patricia Owens. He stared at the words on the screen, not actually seeing them.

Just after 5:30 a.m. Colin tapped him on the shoulder. "Dude, your battery is dead. Didn't you hear it beep?"

He had fallen asleep almost as soon as he sat at the table. He sipped from his coffee, wincing like he had just drunk sour milk.

"Cold," he said.

"You want me to get you another one?" Colin asked.

"Thanks, that would be great."

Roland shut his computer off and stowed it in the case. Just then, Colin placed a fresh coffee on the table. Roland handed him a five and said, "Keep the change."

"Thanks, dude."

Tim's coffee in hand, computer over his shoulder, Roland returned to the B&B and went straight to his room. The lamp in the corner was on, and the bed had been made. Not even 6:00 a.m. and the old woman had already made up his room.

Roland tossed his laptop on the bed, set his half-empty coffee on the nightstand and undressed. His shoulders and neck ached from the two-hour nap on the hard plastic chair at Tim Hortons. His ass wasn't in very good shape either. How could a person toss and turn in a perfectly comfortable bed, and sleep like a baby in a molded plastic torture chair?

He needed a shower, even if it was only to loosen up his aching muscles.

Yes, a shower was exactly what he needed.

Chapter 50

Smoke rose up to the clouds. Every person within ten miles would be able to see it. They all came. They are sure that our problems are behind us. They want to believe that all the demons were in that barn. I am not as sure.

"Anyone who happened on the scene of the fire that day would have thought it quite odd. A dozen people looking at a burning barn. Any other time we all would have been forming a bucket brigade. Trying our best to douse the flames, or at the very least, attempting to minimize the damage.

"We didn't do that though. I stood with Auntie and Bernhard, feeling sad for the people that once were. I'm sure the screams we heard came from voices I once knew. I remember trying to tell myself that they were finally achieving some peace. What a dreadful way to find peace."

Patricia and Roland sat on the porch swing. The morning sun sparkled off the wet grass. An early morning shower left a brilliant rainbow behind, but neither Roland nor Patricia gave it anything more than the mildest of consideration.

"How did word of the fire get around?" Roland asked.

"As I said, the smoke could be seen for miles," she said. "Back then, whenever you saw smoke like that you went to see if you could help.

People showed up with empty buckets, but those buckets ended up being stools to sit on while we watched the end of the plague."

"It wasn't the end, was it?"

"No, Roland. We won a battle, but the war was far from over. Bernhard cautioned me not to be too satisfied. He was sure these individuals were just a fraction of the vampires in Kings Shore. He couldn't say how he knew, but he was positive the source of the monsters, the one who started all of this, was not in that barn."

"Did he think so based on instinct, or past experience?" Roland knew better than to insinuate any skepticism in his tone, but sometimes he couldn't help it. Patricia didn't falter. She just continued, knowing that he would catch up just around the next turn. Of course, he always did.

"It took most of the day for the flames to die down to smoldering embers. We couldn't risk a windy night blowing the hot coals into the forest. The last thing we needed was a forest fire. There was a well behind the barn. It wasn't long before people were taking turns drawing water from the well. We passed the buckets along the line and drenched the smoldering ashes. White steam billowed up from each bucket of water thrown.

"The smell was dreadful. It was a wet smell, but always the underlying stench of the monsters reminded all of us that this was no ordinary blaze. Something evil died in this place.

"It took hours to put enough water on those embers to cool them down. The water just boiled off as soon as it landed in the ashes. It was still steaming and smoldering when we left, but the people were exhausted and hungry and we had to get inside before dark."

She paused there, looking north, as if maybe just speaking of it could rekindle the flames and the black smoke would any second breach the treetops, calling the residents of Kings Shore into action.

When no smoke appeared, Patricia stood and walked to the door. "Let's see if we can't dig up a snack."

Chapter 51

After lunch, Patricia and Roland retired to the parlor. When she was comfortable in her chair, Roland went back to the kitchen to retrieve the drinks. As always, Patricia had a tray set up with fresh glasses. He opened the fridge to find the crystal pitcher.

"Purple," he said to himself. "I guess grape is the flavor of the day."

He loaded it onto the tray with the glasses, all the while wondering how she managed to be so prepared. She always had a jug of some beverage waiting, and the tray was always set with fresh glasses and on some occasions, cookies or crackers. He had yet to see her get these things ready, but somehow she always did.

"So," he said entering the parlor with the tray. "What happened after the fire?"

Patricia motioned to the pitcher without answering. He filled a glass and handed it to her. She sipped some grape juice then set it on the table.

"Sorry, Roland," she said. "My throat was too parched to speak."

"Take your time," he said, sitting on the couch across from her. "I am here until the story is told."

She sat quietly looking out the window, periodically sipping juice. Roland studied her for a moment, trying without success to get inside her head. Her face gave nothing away. The big-shot reporter was going to have to wait for her to tell the tale. Her eyes divulged no secrets.

"Just about every emotion people can have came out at that fire," Patricia said, her head shaking as though she still could not believe what she saw. "Some were actually giddy, dancing and rough-housing. A few cried, thinking their loss had been avenged, while others were still angry.

"A few asked us if we knew who was in there. They looked at us with such hope. Hope that their loved ones weren't in there. Maybe, hope that they were and their ordeal was over.

"Of course we had to tell them that we didn't know who was in the barn, aside from John Moore anyway.

"Some people said John Moore got what he deserved, after what he did to Jacob Hebert. Bernhard would not allow that kind of talk. He told them that nobody deserved what happened that day. He told them that John Moore didn't die in that barn. The devil's servants perished in that barn. John Moore had died days before. He was a fine man, and he didn't deserve what happened to him any more than Jacob did."

"What were you feeling?" Roland asked her.

Patricia wiped a tear from her cheek. He reached across the table, placing his hand on hers.

"At first I was happy that we might have ended the nightmare," she said. "After I saw the look in Bernhard's eyes, I knew that things would get worse before they got better.

"Then, I was afraid. Afraid that I might not survive the summer. Afraid for those people who thought the plague was over. Nobody wants to believe the worst. Those were the people who would be at greatest risk, the ones who thought we would be fine after the fire, I mean. Bernhard knew that, and I knew it too. As if he could read my thoughts, Bernhard tried to caution everyone. He tried to tell them that this was not the end of the horror. We knew some fools wouldn't listen. We knew people would go back to their old ways. We knew that people would die when the sun dipped below the horizon."

"Did you come back here after the fire?" Roland asked.

"Only long enough to get a few things and close up the house. Then we went back to Auntie's."

"What was it like in town?"

"Worse than we feared," she said. "The men were walking around the street drunk. They were shouting and laughing. Some were shooting guns into the air. Bernhard only shook his head and went inside."

"'When the sun sets,' Bernhard said, 'the vampires will feed and some of those fools out there will be turned into demons before morning. Then it will be our job to kill them.'

"After that, he went to Auntie's guest room and slammed the door.

"I remember looking out the window. Those men were so happy. It was like New Year's Eve in the summer. The women had more sense, or maybe they were still too frightened to be in the street. All the revelers in the street were young men.

"Just before dusk, a couple of those men were dragged off by their women.

Those were the lucky ones."

"I bet they didn't think so at the time," Roland said after sipping some juice.

Chapter 52

Patricia's Journal—Tuesday, July 9, 1912

Bernhard was right. Oh, how I wish he was not. They came back. I didn't think they could feel anything but hunger. I know better now. The demons can feel anger.

Patricia decided it was time for her afternoon stroll, and Roland was more than happy to comply. It wasn't that he was uncomfortable, but he needed to get up and move around.

When they stepped into the sun, Patricia took hold of his arm to stop him.

"Young man," she said. "Do you think that fancy car of yours can take us to the beach? I would dearly love to see the lake."

Roland was completely taken by surprise.

"That, my good lady, is a capital idea."

Roland guided her to the passenger side of the car and opened the door. Holding his hand for support, Patricia lowered herself into the Bimmer's leather seat.

She didn't say anything on the ride. She just admired the leather interior and marveled at the German finishing. She ran her fingers over the dash and the seams on the upholstery.

Content to enjoy the beautiful day and the peaceful drive, Roland chose not to prod her for details of what he was sure would be a true horror story.

Maybe, Patricia chose to take a drive to the beach because she wanted to postpone telling the story, or she needed the inspiration the lake brought to get her through it.

Whatever the reason, they were not disappointed. With Patricia's instructions, Roland parked the car on a stretch of pristine, deserted beach on the shore of Lake Huron. Lining the shore were miles of algae-coated rocks worn smooth by centuries of erosion. Standing at the water's edge, Roland was stunned by the beauty of this place. He had no idea that the Great Lakes could look so clean.

"Wow," he uttered.

"Roland," she said. "I have visited this place thousands of times, and I feel that way every time."

"I have never seen water as clear as this," he said.

"They don't like water," she said. "The vampires."

"They can't swim?"

"Sink like they were made of iron," she said with a chuckle.

"Can they drown?"

"No, they don't die," she said. "They're dead already. If one of them fell off a boat in the middle of the lake, it would sink to the bottom. Eventually, it would come to shore. I think they just walk on the bottom."

"Jesus," he mumbled.

"Jesus did not visit Kings Shore in the summer of 1912," she said.

She reached for Roland's hand. They walked along the shore, holding hands while she told him what happened after sunset.

"Bernhard tried without success to get those fools to get inside. He stormed out of Auntie's guest room and almost ran out to the town common.

"'They're all dead,' Jack Bronson told Bernhard. 'You killed them in that fire.'

"Jack was a foreman at Daddy's mill for a while, but he got fired when he showed up at work drunk." Patricia laughed out loud. "That fool tried to punch Daddy in the nose when he got fired. Daddy put him on the seat of his pants before he could say, 'Oh shoot.'"

"I wish I could have met your father," Roland said.

She squeezed his hand and continued, "Auntie shouted from the porch for Bernhard to get inside. The sun was so low in the sky. Bernhard made one last plea, but Jack and his group just shooed Bernhard away like he was an annoying bug."

Patricia stopped walking and looked into the water. Roland looked to see what she was watching.

"You see the sunfish?"

Roland didn't see anything but the slimy rocks in the water. He was sure she was stalling. Patricia took more of these moments, as her tale grew more gruesome. She wasn't just telling a story. Patricia was reliving it. Nobody should witness the horror that plagued this community, and this poor old woman was living it a second time.

"Bernhard came into Auntie's just minutes before things went bad. We looked out the window, watching and hoping Bernhard was wrong."

"He wasn't wrong though," Roland said, trying to help her say what she didn't want to say.

Chapter 53

Patricia and Roland continued along the beach at a pace that would normally drive him to frustration. That was the old Roland. This Roland held her hand in his and assisted her progress over the rocky shore.

She made small talk for a while, pointing to birds and a coyote, and voicing concern over how much trash people tossed into the lake.

"When I walked here as a girl, the lake didn't have anything in it that wasn't supposed to be."

Her voice quavered slightly, and Roland's concern for his new friend began to consume his thoughts. He swore he could see the lines on her face deepen while they talked, and hear the strength in her voice falter.

"I didn't have the privilege of knowing Bernhard for very long, but during that short time I never knew him to be wrong." She shifted gears without a hitch. One second she editorialized on the careless way today's youth treated the environment, and the next she was back in 1912.

Patricia stumbled on the uneven ground, and she almost fell to the rocks. If Roland hadn't been holding her hand, she surely would have. He heard a slight moan from her as his grip tightened to keep her up. Once she regained her balance, Roland immediately released her, fearing he may have injured her hand in the process of protecting her.

If she was hurt, she gave him no indication and continued where she left off.

"The scene that unfolded before us that night could only be called surreal. Those men, drunkenly defiant, scoffed at the obvious danger they were in. "Without warning, the bandstand was surrounded by six vampires. They didn't advance on the men there. They just stood around them, watching them as though those men were the most interesting show on earth.

"'Go back where you came from, demons, before we incinerate you as well,' Jack said.

Patricia said, "One of the men tossed a cigarette at the feet of one of the creatures, and they all ran off. Jack and his cohorts thought that very funny. They guffawed loud enough for the whole town to hear. A door opened across the street. Bernhard yelled to stay inside, and the door slammed shut again.

"That was when we heard the sound. At first, we thought sure it was a woman's footsteps. You know that light clicking sound a woman's heels make on a hard surface?"

Roland nodded.

"It was like that, but it was no woman. The thing that made those footsteps was neither woman nor man. Oh, I'm sure it was a man once, but that day had long passed. It was the size of a man. It wore clothes like a man, albeit clothes from an earlier time."

Roland struggled to imagine how old-fashioned clothes had to be for Patricia to make that statement.

"It dressed like something from a Dickens play. A tattered overcoat hung limp on the thing's frame. Saggy, grey woolen trousers met boots with big brass buckles on them. The boot leather had no shine left, but those buckles shone so brilliant, they bordered on luminescent. He even wore a top-hat, can you imagine?"

Roland couldn't but only shook his head.

"'What the hell are you?' Jack scoffed.

"Those were Jack's last words," Patricia continued. "That thing snatched Jack by the Adam's apple, and before he knew what was happening, that vampire tore Jack's throat out. He stood gaping at the monster in dis-belief for a moment, his hands trying in vain to staunch the deluge from his throat. Jack fell to his knees a moment later. We could hear him making a sickly gargling sound as his lungs filled with his own blood.

"In seconds the creatures that ran away earlier were back, lapping up every drop of spilled blood as it cascaded down the steps of the bandstand.

"The other men with Jack were not laughing anymore. They tried to run, but three more vampires appeared between those men and shelter.

"They played with those men, like cats toying with a mouse they had no desire to eat. Their screams for help echoed through the town for what seemed like an eternity.

"The one that killed Jack walked over and stood directly in front of Auntie's door. It knew. Somehow that dreadful demon knew that it was Bernhard who set that fire. It still wore that ridiculous top-hat so we couldn't see its face. The brim of the hat cast shadows down to the creature's chin."

Patricia sat shaking her head, trying to prevent herself from visualizing that night. She closed her eyes, her face wrinkling like an old balloon as she squeezed her eyes shut with the effort, but the images came. Somehow, tears began to trickle from her pinched lids.

"His hands," she said. "We couldn't see his face, but the hands were clearly exposed to the glow from fires and the moonlight. They were not the hands of a human. Oh, they had the general shape of hands, but they looked like the talons of a raptor. The fingers were too long and God-awful. The knuckles were over-pronounced, the skin was pale, on the verge of being transparent. Black veins crisscrossed the back of those hands.

"Just when I was thinking, if the hands look that awful, I'm glad I can't see the monster's face, it raised one of those hands to the brim of the hat.

"I am not ashamed to say that I swooned when that thing removed the hat. I will never forget how ghastly it was. It had pointed ears like a bat on the sides of a completely bald head. Eyes, Roland. You can't imagine the evil pools that were in the place where his eyes should have been. Deep black pools of evil. It had a long narrow face with a hook of a nose and a slit for a mouth.

"It grinned at us. That was when I fainted. It had a mouth full of jagged teeth. It looked more like the mouth of a shark than a man."

Chapter 54

Roland sat alone in his room at the B&B. He sat back in the wing chair, his arms crossed over his chest. He stared at his recorder almost as though he were afraid to push the play button. Long shadows ran the length of the room as the early evening sun dipped ever closer to the horizon.

A knock on the door caused him to jump to his feet.

"Who is it?" Roland said to the closed door.

"Mr. Millhouse?" a small voice replied.

Roland opened the door to find Mrs. Parent, the proprietor of the B&B, standing in the hall. Just barely five feet tall, Mrs. Parent had to crane her neck straight up to look into Roland's eyes. Dressed in night-clothes, it was obvious that Mrs. Parent was ready for bed.

"Mr. Millhouse, can I get you anything before I go to bed?"

"No thank you, Mrs. Parent. I'm fine. You have a good night."

"You do the same, Mr. Millhouse. Instead of clicking away on that computer of yours, might I suggest you go to sleep as well. You're looking a bit run down."

"I'm just a little tired," he assured her. "I just have a little work to finish up, and then I promise I will call it a night."

Mrs. Parent didn't say anything, she just cocked her right eyebrow. It was a gesture Roland knew to mean, I don't believe you.

"Cross my heart, Mrs. Parent. As soon as I finish this up, I will go right to sleep." Roland felt like he was making a justification to his mother to stay up late in order to finish his homework.

She gave him another brief glance, then turned and walked away. Roland closed the door and looked to his recorder. His shoulders slumped, and he made his way back to the armchair. He reached for the machine and pushed Play.

Patricia's voice filled the room as though she were sitting there with him.

"What is that?" I asked Bernhard when I regained myself.

"That, Miss Owens, is the one we must find. It is the source of all the evil that inhabits your little village."

Bernhard's face was a picture of conviction when he uttered those words. It didn't matter how many vampires we burned up. If we didn't find and kill that one, our problems would never be gone.

I looked through the window when my legs felt steady enough to hold me up. I saw only an empty street. Over on the bandstand the corpses of those poor idiot men lay as a grotesque warning to all of us. The leader of the vampires left them that way to tell us that he was in charge.

"I don't think we will see any more trouble from them tonight," Bernhard said. "We should try to get some sleep. We will need to resume the hunt for its resting place as soon as it is light. Until we find it, we are all in grave danger."

Auntie passed around glasses of sherry. I never did acquire a taste for it and waved her off. Bernhard drank his down in a gulp and held his glass out for a refill. Bernhard and Auntie stayed up until the bottle was empty.

Maybe I should have forced myself to drink the sherry. Bernhard and Auntie slept past sunrise. I should know, I didn't sleep a wink. I tossed in that bed for hours, but once I was certain that Auntie and Bernhard were not going to stir, I went back downstairs. I sat in a chair and stared out that same window.

Of course, Bernhard was right. He always was. The demons didn't come back. If you could discount the corpses out there, it was a quiet, beautiful evening in Kings Shore.

I sat in the dark that night. When the sun breached the horizon and began to flood the room with light, I noticed something that brought the whole dreadful night back.

The wall and floor around the front door remained bloodstained. Bernhard had removed Jacob's detached head from the room, but nobody cleaned up the blood. Or maybe that blood couldn't be cleaned with a single cleaning.

When Bernhard found me that morning, I was scrubbing the walls and floor. The water in the pail didn't look like water anymore. It had a pink tinge. Bernhard took the pail away, leaving me on my knees in front of the door. When he came back, he carried a bucket of fresh water.

Bernhard and Auntie were preparing breakfast when I finished scrubbing the blood away. We ate eggs and toast. I don't remember any of us uttering a single word during that meal. Every clink and scrape those knives and forks made against the china plates sounded amplified in the ominous silence of that morning. Not a single sound came in from the open windows either. Deafening is the only way to describe a community as silent.

Chapter 55

Patricia's Journal—Thursday, July 11, 1912

A day of chaos. The countryside looked like hell on earth.

Satan's furnace had erupted in the countryside. Everywhere you looked, plumes of smoke etched a ghastly image against the blue sky. The smell of burning wood and fabrics turned the very act of breathing into an affront.

Roland sat at a table at Tim's reading over the notes he had typed on his computer earlier.

A group of riot-incensed maniacs decided to expedite the vampire hunt of 1912 by setting fire to every abandoned home and barn in the county. They wasted so much time trying to put the fires out, or at best, prevent them from spreading to the forest, that no vampire nests were found.

As the sun sank below the horizon on the far side of Lake Huron, we were exhausted. Not a single monster died, and they would be coming into town to feed. Bernhard had left me behind with Auntie to build teepee fires along Main Street. Just before sunset, they were ignited. It looked almost like daytime out there for a while. Eventually, the fires burned out, and when they did, the demons came.

They were very cautious at first. They stayed clear of the fires even when the fires were not much more than smoldering embers. We got another demonstration why when a gust of wind swirled up some embers. Before we knew what happened, the one closest to the fire in front of the general store burst into flames.

It screamed one of those ear-splitting howls of agony, then calmed down. After the initial writhing, it just stood there, white flames consuming it. Black smoke filled the air. I was grateful to be downwind that night. Breathing that foulness once was once too often.

Just like the previous night, they gathered around the burning thing until it was completely consumed by the flames. Just like the last time they kept at a safe distance. I still have trouble imagining those demons having feelings, but they did seem to mourn the passing of their brethren.

Eventually, they left the smoldering ashes and wandered up and down the street. They looked in windows, and sometimes they leaped onto the roofs. I often think how terrifying it was to have one of them climbing around on the roof above me.

Nobody went to bed. I could see lights on up and down the street. A few people were brave enough to pull their curtains aside and look out. Most, I think, were cowering in their basements or in closets. Maybe some hid under beds like frightened children.

Bernhard was a dervish that night, going from room to room, looking through windows, making notes on every vampire he saw.

About an hour before dawn, the monsters turned and walked north on Main, disappearing into the dark. Such a surreal sight, it was almost as though the things had been summoned, and were powerless to resist.

I heard no noise, but you would swear they were called away. Maybe the demon in the top-hat stood in the shadows where he couldn't be seen. I think they could see much better in the dark than we could. So it could have been that.

He remembered Patricia struggling with how to describe the way they communicated. "They did have some kind of, what is it called? When you can make people hear what you are thinking without saying it?

"Clairvoyance?" Roland asked.

"Yes," she said. "Maybe the old one could just think it, and they would leave. Whatever the reason, it was eerie."

Chapter 56

Roland pulled the Bimmer up to the front step of the old mansion. A foreboding grey sky had blotted out the glorious weather that Roland and Patricia had enjoyed to this point in his stay.

Roland looked to the sky and frowned. Not because he dreaded the onset of rain. Patricia's story thus far had dragged him into a funk, and he took the sour turn in weather as a sign that things would only get worse. Things would surely get much worse.

"I think we had better stay close to home today. Don't you think?" Patricia said, as she pushed open the old door.

Roland looked up with alarm at the frail sound of her voice. She must have noticed. With some effort, a smile blossomed on her face, easing his concern a bit.

"I think you may have a point," Roland said, trotting up the steps to stand at her side.

They stood on the porch for a moment studying the overcast morning like a pair of amateur meteorologists.

"What do you think, young man?" she said. "Shall we stay out here, or retire to the parlor?"

"Out here, I think," Roland said, motioning her to the wicker chairs. "Would you like me to get anything before we sit?"

"Dear boy," she said through a giggle, "you know what to do."

"Indeed I do." He walked her to her seat. She held his arm as she lowered herself to the cushion. Roland returned to the door, and just as he swung it open, Scuba jumped onto Patricia's lap and curled up on her brown polyester-covered legs. With a smile and a shake of his head, Roland went inside.

In the kitchen, Roland found a familiar scene. Patricia had set a tray with tea and cookies. Everything was ready to be served. He reached for the tray, and his left hand brushed her journal lying on the counter. A chill surged up his arm, and he recoiled as though he'd been shocked.

"Jesus," he said through a gasp.

Being careful not to touch the book again, Roland picked up the tray and returned to the front porch. Placing the tray on the table between the two chairs, he looked to Patricia.

She was off in that place again. A few days ago, he wished he could go with her to her place, but after a few nightmares, Patricia's mind was the last place he ever wanted to look into.

Roland poured tea from the floral-print pot into the matching cups, dropped a sugar cube in each, and added a lemon wedge. Scuba watched his every move while he worked. He took the seat next to Patricia and waited for her to come back.

The grey morning ushered in a drizzle that hung in the air like fog. Roland looked out toward the road, but visibility was limited to the sickly bushes that dominated the landscape of Patricia's yard.

Not a breath of wind disturbed the mist. Droplets of water gathered on the porch railing. In a while, the moisture on the railing gathered enough to begin dripping. Scuba saw that as a sign of things to come and hopped off Patricia's lap and sauntered over to the door.

"Like a rat leaving a sinking ship, do you think?" she mused. Then added, "Be a dear and let Scuba into the house. I don't think he wants to listen to our chat. Scuba scurried through the door without delay, and before Roland could close it, Patricia asked him if he would mind retrieving her journal.

With more than a little dread, he did as asked.

Chapter 57

Patricia's Journal—July 12, 1912

We can't keep this up much longer. No one in town has slept. Maybe that is their plan. If they keep us up all night, how can we hunt them during the day? We slept most of the day away. No monsters were found today. I dread the sunset.

After she read this passage, Patricia went back to her place. She must feel safer there, Roland thought. Her journal hung loosely from her hands, and he retrieved it and placed it on the table next to the tray.

"Roland," Patricia said coming out of her trance. "I think I need to go inside. Would you give me a hand?"

"Are you alright?" he asked. His eyes were wide and bored into her. His immediate reaction was concern. This wasn't like her at all. "Should I call someone?"

"You know," Patricia said with a weak grin. "I think maybe you should call my physician. His card is in a card-thingy on the desk in the study. Help me to my room, then give Mark a call. That's his name, Dr. Mark Dalton. He is a sweet boy, just like you, dear."

Roland paced outside Patricia's room while the doctor checked her condition. Not a sound interrupted the steady plodding of his Reeboks on the hardwood floor.

When her bedroom door opened, Roland stopped short. "Well, how is she?"

"For a woman of 120 years, she is surprisingly good," Dr. Dalton said.

"To be breathing at that age is an accomplishment," Roland replied. "But, how is she? When I met her just days ago, she could have passed for a young seventy-five. She seems to have aged twenty years in that time."

"Yes," the young doctor agreed. "It does concern me that she has declined this rapidly, but there is little we can do. I would like to say she is a bit under the weather, but my gut tells me her body has finally decided to get old."

"That's all you got," Roland said, doing his best to stifle the urge to yell at this man. "She is getting old."

"If it were anyone else, I would advise her family to make sure her affairs are in order. But Miss Owens has defied pretty much all that we know about aging, so I wouldn't be surprised to hear that she got out of bed tomorrow and took her morning walk to the cemetery."

"She has no family," Roland said.

"I know," Dr. Dalton replied. "I have advised her many times about naming someone as power of attorney. Her solicitor tells me she finally did just that, two days ago."

Roland tried to think. He was with her every day, and nobody had been to the house but him. The only time she would have had to make arrangements like that was when he had gone back to the B&B.

"You must have made some impression on her, Mr. Millhouse."

"I'm sorry?"

"Miss Owens has named you as her power of attorney in all matters. Her financial and medical decisions are up to you, should she become incapacitated."

"Me?"

Mark Dalton looked him over like he might a used car. It was the kind of scrutiny every stranger got when they came into a small town. Roland looked down at his clothes, he was sure he had a stain on his shirt, or maybe the fly on his cargo shorts was down. Satisfied that his appearance met his own standards, Roland returned his gaze to Mark.

"She asked me to send you in," Dalton said. "I will let myself out." With that, Dr. Dalton walked past Roland and out of the house.

Chapter 58

Roland stood in front of the old wooden door. He knew she was waiting for him, but he couldn't decide if he should knock or just enter.

"Roland, are you there?" came a small voice from behind the closed door.

He reached for the ornate brass knob and pushed the door open just far enough to peer into the room. Dr. Dalton had drawn the drapes, leaving the room filled with shadows.

"Come in, Roland," Patricia called from her bed. "And be a dear and let some daylight in here. I don't know what it is about doctors. Before long, I will be spending eternity in complete darkness. There is no point rushing it along. Wouldn't you say?"

"I learned very early on not to argue with you," Roland said, hustling over to the window.

"You're a smart boy. A fast learner, we used to say. You will make some young lady a fine husband."

While Patricia was praising him, Roland had made his way around the room, opening the drapes on two walls. The dreary clouds had moved off, and brilliant rays of warmth streamed into the room.

"Ah, that's better. Don't you think so, Roland?"

Roland nodded then asked, "Is there anything else I can do for you."

Patricia was sitting up, big frilly pillows bunched up around her. Her cheeks had the glow Roland had come to recognize from the time he first met her. Her eyes were wide open and sparkled in the afternoon light.

"The young doctor has forbade me getting out of bed today, so we are going to have our chat in here. So, if you would, run down to the kitchen and bring us some lemonade and cookies. You know where everything is. Then, when you return, pull one of those chairs close to the bed so I don't have to yell across the room."

Roland did as instructed, and about twenty minutes later he sat in an armchair at Patricia's bedside.

"As I mentioned downstairs," she began, "the day had been lost as far as finding any more of the monsters. Bernhard took on an obsession with that ugly bald thing. He was sure it was the source of all the evil in Kings Shore, and if we could find and kill it, the others would either leave or be easy to dispose of. That was how he phrased it. Dispose of."

Roland poured some lemonade and handed a glass to her. The ice cubes clinked against the glass as she took it in her shaky hand and raised it to her lips. Roland handed her a napkin, and she dabbed the moisture from her lips as he took the glass from her and placed it back on the night-stand.

"Maybe we should take a day off," Roland said.

"Nonsense," she said, waving away his gesture as silly.

"The darkness in the street that night was like none I can remember seeing, before or since," she continued "There was no time to build the fires like we did the night before, and clouds had completely obscured what little moonlight might have come from that sliver of light we had seen the previous night." Roland tried to give her the lemonade, but she shook her head.

"They didn't come right away. I have to admit I began to hope for the best. That just maybe they left, or even better, died out there in the woods. Bernhard didn't entertain such thoughts. He paced from room to room, scanning the street through slits in the curtains, squinting through the darkness.

"I must say, I got the feeling that he could actually see in the dark.

About two hours after sunset, Bernhard yelled through the closed window, 'Get inside you fool.' It was Tami." Patricia paused, squeezing her eyes shut. "Oh, I can't remember the girl's last name.

"Isn't that silly? She was the prettiest girl in town. She was a year older than I was. We had gone to school together for years. She was loved by the men and reviled by the women. It wasn't her fault she was so pretty, so I didn't hold it against her. Tami had a smile that could light up a room. Unfortunately, few men saw her smile. That girl had the highest, perkiest bosom you could imagine.

"I guess Tami let herself believe what I could only hope. That the monsters had moved on. She stepped out on her porch, to have a look down the street. She stood with a lantern extended out to the darkness.

"She never saw them coming. Two vampires dropped onto her porch from nowhere. I heard screams from across the road. Not from Tami. It came from one of the windows. The voice sounded familiar to me but at the time I was so concerned for Tami, I didn't let the voice all the way in.

"Tami looked stunned at first, like she didn't understand what was happening to her. Then her eyes took on a euphoric look. I am as sure as you are sitting here now, that Tami was enjoying the experience. Then her eyes drifted shut, and a moment later the two demons released her, and she fell to the ground.

"When she fell her lantern erupted in flames, and one of the things didn't get out of the way in time. I just turned away from the window. I had seen enough of that macabre sight.

"After a while, I rejoined Bernhard and Auntie at the window. The thing was still smoldering in the street. The dreadful smell had wafted into the house. I thought I would be sick from it.

"It might be said that Tami gave her life to kill one of them, but that isn't how it turned out. Her lantern didn't just burn up a vampire. Her porch ignited. Then the whole house went up. Three people were in the house that night. Tami's father, and his brother. We will never know if they knew Tami had gone outside, but when that house started to burn, they ran into the street.

"Bernhard yelled at them to carry some fire, but they fled the fire in panic. It was impossible to tell how many vampires there were. To me it felt like every time I laid eyes on one of them, it was the first time. Bernhard told me they can get into our heads and make us forget their faces. That is why he took notes. So he could try to get a count."

Patricia motioned to her glass, and Roland handed it to her. Her hand now steady, had no sign of the tremor. She sipped some lemonade, and Roland put it back on the nightstand for her.

"Do you need to rest?" he asked.

She didn't reply. Patricia just closed her eyes. Roland raised himself from the chair as gently as he could manage, and left the room, pulling the door closed behind him.

chapter 59

Three hours later, Roland returned from town with soup and sandwiches from the deli. He expected to take a tray up to her room, but Patricia was sitting on the porch.

"I guess you are feeling better," he said.

"I am." She pointed at the bags and said, "What do you have there?"

"Soup and sandwiches. I got you beef barley and egg salad. I hope that is okay? The girl at the deli told me it was your favorite."

"Aneska?" Patricia asked. When he shrugged, indicating he had no idea what her name was, she added, "A pretty girl, dark skin, twenty-three years old?"

"That sounds like her."

"She is a doll, Roland. The next time you see her, you should really introduce yourself."

"Miss Owens, are you trying to play matchmaker?" he said with a grin.

"I'm just saying you aren't getting any younger. Do you want to be 120 years old some day and be all alone?"

When their laughter trailed off, Roland said, "Patricia, I am not sure I want to live that long."

"I can't blame you for that. I have had good health, but I have been to more funerals than I can count. Over the years I had many friends. I always volunteered to watch over those children when the mommas and daddies needed a break. Since I had no children of my own, I was happy to do it. When the little ones I watched over began to die from old age, I knew I had seen more than my share of years. I would have loved to have a few of my own, but I surely would have attended their funerals by now. How dreadful would that have been?"

"I can't agree with you more," he said. "Shall we go into the dining room for some lunch?"

"That sounds wonderful."

"Just let me carry these in and I will come back to escort you inside like a lady should be," Roland said with a wink. He tried to make light of it, but what he really meant was, don't get up until I can help you.

They didn't discuss the spring of 1912 while they ate. Patricia continued to encourage Roland to befriend Aneska. She filled him in on a few other young women in town who, as far as she knew, were single.

Roland told her about some of the new projects going on in town, most notably, the splash pad going in behind the bandstand.

"What say you go relax in the parlor while I tidy up in here?" Roland said. He phrased it as a question, but they both understood it to be an instruction.

When Roland joined her in the parlor, Patricia had her journal in her lap. He set the tray he was carrying on the coffee table and poured her a cup of tea.

"It's very hot, so you had better let it sit a while," he warned her.

Satisfied that Patricia was comfortable, Roland sat across from her and gestured to her book.

Without a word, she opened her journal.

Patricia's Journal—Saturday, July 13, 1912

It was worse than I feared. Hell rose up from the depths of Hades, and the breath of Satan burns so. Many more from town were taken, my friend Tami among them.

"The fire that burned Tami's house had spread. The house next door was empty, but there was a tavern next to that, and believe it or not, the tavern did a brisk business that night. At least until the fire."

"Talk about dying to get a drink," Roland said.

Patricia nodded. "That is exactly the way I thought of it then."

"Ten men came running from that building. The first six were taken. The other four managed to run off. One man chose to stay in the tavern. We could see him through the window. Silhouetted against the glass, the fire burned bright behind him. He feared death by fire less than death by demon. I think the smoke took him long before the flames. He disappeared from the window, but didn't cry out."

"So you were certain there were at least six of them," Roland said.

"Seven," Patricia corrected. "The bald monster did not join them. He walked into town a bit later, just as casual as you please, and stood on the street right in front of Auntie's door dressed in that same odd attire."

"Did it speak?" Roland asked.

"Not like you and I are speaking now. We could hear it inside our head, but not with our ears. It seemed to know that Bernhard was the biggest threat in town.

"Do you know what that little man did next?" she said with a giggle.

Roland shrugged.

"He began to sing. I don't know the song. He sang it in German. I gathered it was a happy song from the melody. The thing was furious. Somehow, Bernhard knew that if he concentrated on singing, it could not get into his head.

"I laughed while he sang. I think the demon became further infuriated by my laughter. That was when we heard the front door. At first, I thought one of them had entered the house. I grabbed one of Bernhard's fire bottles, and rushed to the door."

Patricia shuddered and raised her hands to cover her face. Roland reached across and put his hand on her shoulder.

"Auntie?" he asked.

She nodded through her sobs. Roland squeezed her shoulder to let her know he was there for her.

"The rain moved out hours ago. Would you like to walk a bit?" he said.

Her hands still over her face, she nodded. Roland retrieved a box of tissues from the end table and placed one in her hand. She dabbed her eyes, tucked the tissue in the pocket of her sweater and extended her hand.

"Doctor's orders be damned," she said, and got up from her chair.

CHAPTER 60

Roland walked along in silence as Patricia recounted that night's events. He had grown to fear her words but found himself powerless to resist their lure.

Before either of us could stop her, Auntie walked through the door as though she were going out to greet an old friend.

"Auntie," I screamed. But she didn't hear me. That thing had her in a spell. She walked right to it. It took her right there while we watched. The thing ripped open her dress.

Isn't it sad, that my first thought was embarrassment for her? That thing wasn't satisfied to take her life, he wanted to degrade her. He wanted to enrage Bernhard so he would run out to save her. We were in the open door, the light spilling out illuminated Auntie's exposed bosom. Bernhard held me back. I was trying to run out to help her. She made the slightest whimper when it bit into her bosom then her head fell back as if she were with a lover.

The monstrous creature looked into my eyes while he drained the life from my last living relation. In that moment, I could see him the way that Auntie saw him when she walked into the street. He was a vision of true beauty. No abomination could ever be more offensive. A monster as ugly as any that has walked the earth, with the power to deceive so convincingly, and with such evil intent, is truly enough to make Jesus himself forsake the lord.

When Auntie went limp, the monster scooped her into its arms and carried her away.

The rest of them followed, leaving the corpses of the six men from the tavern, and the charred remains of the three from Tami's. By then the smoldering vampire had been reduced to a black stain on the road.

Patricia's Journal—Sunday, July 14, 1912

I am completely alone in the world. I have no family. God, why have you let Satan consume my family? Does my faith need such a test? If You think yes, then I have failed.

My faith has been lost.

I sat all that night in Bernhard's arms. I rocked back and forth on the couch, and he rocked with me. The dear man never wavered in his support. I think we both slept off and on.

As soon as the sun breached the horizon, Bernhard began the day. The most immediate task, to dispose of the dead. Just like all the others, a grave was dug in the cemetery, the body went in and was soaked with kerosene. After those who wished to give their last respects came forward, the bodies were torched. The smell, oh how awful.

The graves were left open until the fires burned out. Bernhard left two men to close the graves when the smoke cleared.

The rest of those left in town were divided into two groups. The vampire hunters, and the childcare workers.

Since I refused to be separated from Bernhard, I went with the vampire hunters. We again went from farm to farm searching for their hiding place.

The day became one disappointment after another. We found several dead animals, horses, cows, goats, and dogs. In the old Miller farm, a hideous thing wandered aimlessly around the house. I think it was a failed attempt to change Mr. Miller into one of them. It was neither human nor vampire. It bumped into walls, and stumbled over furniture.

"Put it out of its misery," Pete Lameraux said.

John Smithson put a bullet in Mr. Miller's brain. He fell to the floor but kept flailing. They shot that man twenty times, and he wouldn't stop. Bernhard pushed through the crowd with an axe. The gunfire stopped when he entered the room. He walked right up to that abomination, and without hesitation, swung the axe, removing Mr. Miller's head.

Moments later the body went still. Two men dragged it outside. Bernhard took a towel from the kitchen and used it to cover the head before he picked it up. Nobody wanted to touch it, and Bernhard was no exception. He tossed the grotesque bundle on top of the corpse and burned it.

Chapter 61

Roland felt better about things when he got Patricia settled back in her bed. Propped up with her pillows, her teacup steaming on the nightstand and her journal in her lap, she was ready to continue.

"When darkness fell over the town that night, I truly envied my Mother and Daddy their peaceful slumber. The monsters came to town in force. Up and down the street they walked, staring into the houses. Dim light shone in every window of every home. Most curtains and shades were pulled tight, but a few brave souls peered out into the darkness.

"Bernhard, as always, prowled the house, peering from window to window. He had more energy than any human I have ever met."

Patricia paused for a moment and looked about the room. The ceiling light and both bedside lamps illuminated the room with pale yellowish light.

"This is quite silly, Roland," she said.

"Sorry?"

"It won't be dark for another two hours, and we have all the windows covered and these dreadful lights on. This part of the house is blessed with a view of the most glorious sunsets in the country.

"Be a dear and pull those blinds, would you?"

He did as asked, and when he looked back to her, her face glowed.

"That's better. If you would, turn the lights off. We don't need them anymore."

With the sun flooding in, the lights did little to brighten the room. When Roland turned them off, it just made the sunlight all the brighter.

"As I was saying," she continued, "Bernhard trundled from one window to the next, looking for the first sign of the vampires.

"That was when the oddest thing happened. I had told Carol about Bernhard's singing. How it seemed to stymie the old one. She must have mentioned it to others.

"Just before midnight, I heard singing coming from the church. Several men and women were still staying in the church at night. They set up a temporary toilet in the pastor's closet. It was just a bucket, with a toilet seat propped on it, but it served them. Well damned if they didn't start singing hymns. By the sound of them, they all sang. It was dreadful singing, and the most glorious sound I have ever heard.

"The scene looked like a replay of the previous night. The vampires strolled up and down the road, looking into windows. I think they were trying to make that mental connection. Trying to lure lazy minds into the street.

"Shortly after the vampires walked into town, I heard singing from the open windows of the nearby houses. It seems the whole town, what was left of us anyway, had taken to song.

"The monsters were infuriated. They began to run up onto porches, and climb walls. They were in a near frenzy when he came. The old one. He held his arms up to the sky, and every last one of them settled down.

"As he did the night before, the old one stood before Auntie's door. He motioned to the north end of town. A ghostly figure emerged from the shadows.

The fires illuminated the skin of a completely naked form."

"Auntie?" Roland asked.

Patricia nodded and continued, "Bernhard had formed a fondness for her, and the old one knew it. I think he felt that Bernhard would charge out of the house to rescue her."

"Bernhard didn't act on emotion though, did he?"

"What he did was go up to a second-floor window, singing that same song the whole time. As soon as Auntie had come close enough, Bernhard set her ablaze with one of his fire bottles.

"Auntie's screams consumed the night. I ran up the stairs to find Bernhard sitting on the floor next to the window. His hands covered his ears, and he wept like a child.

"I wanted to scream at him, to demand he tell me how he could do that to Auntie. All I could do is walk to the window, and look down at the flaming form of my last family member. My vision blurred through the tears as I watched the white flames end all hope that maybe she could be found before she became one of them.

"When her screams stopped, Auntie turned and faced him, the old one that brought this plague to our town. He looked up at me standing in the window. I have never seen such hate before. His gaze burned into me. In that moment, I wanted to jump out of the window to be with him."

Patricia's whole body quaked as the memory of that moment sent a shudder through her.

"Bernhard came out of his grieving with an anger that equaled what I saw in the eyes of that thing. He saw me leaning toward the open window and shoved me away. He didn't mean to use such force, but in the heat of the moment, we can't always control our bodies. I went sprawling to the floor. My head banged against the wall so hard I almost lost consciousness."

"'Your time here is at an end,' Bernhard yelled down at the old one.

"When I got back to the window, the hideous face smiled up at us. Then he turned and looked to Auntie, and pointed to the church. Auntie began to stagger toward the church. The white flames lit the street like midday. I knew the church had many people in it, and I called for her to stop.

"Auntie didn't stop until her body had been all but turned to ash. That wasn't soon enough, however. Auntie collapsed on the steps of the church. The whole thing had been constructed of wood. In seconds the front of the church looked like the gates of hell."

Patricia shook her head as the images she described came back to her.

"The singing from the church turned to screams of terror. Chairs came flying through the stained-glass windows at the side of the church, followed by dozens of panic-stricken men, women, and children.

"They seemed safe at first. The vampires wouldn't go near the flames. As the fire spread through the building, the heat forced the people into the street. They didn't know what to do at first. Bernhard tossed one of his fire bottles at the old one.

"He dodged it quite easily, and that demon yelled out, as clear as can be, 'I will leave here when I say it is time to leave.'"

Chapter 62

"They came from everywhere. Even Bernhard was taken by surprise at the number of them. Fifteen, maybe twenty vampires emerged from the shadows. They looked like men, women, and children, but they were lethal monsters. Every one of them, a killing machine, hell-bent on death.

"One of the women from the church, Mrs. Peters, saw her son come out of the darkness. She ran to the boy, and he took her. As Maureen Davidson had been taken by her son, so was Mrs. Peters.

"The rest of them, the people from the church, ran. The old one took Carol. I screamed at that demon to leave her be.

"He stopped for a moment, just long enough to look up to the window where I stood. He smiled, and I could see Carol's blood glistening on those jagged teeth.

"Bernhard tried again to set him ablaze with one of his fire bottles, but the thing again evaded the flames with ease. He dragged Carol along with him, drank from her until she went limp in his arms and then he heaved her at us. What a dreadful sound it was when poor Carol's body crashed against the side of the building."

When Patricia paused, Roland asked, "Do you need to rest?"

"All this talking has made me terrible thirsty," she said. "Do you think you can get us something to drink?"

When Roland returned to her room, Patricia sat in her bed, her face as blank as a new sheet of paper. She appeared to be looking out the window, but Roland knew she had gone to her refuge. A place deep inside her mind where nothing bad ever happened and evil could not go.

He set the tray on the table near her bed and poured them each a glass of iced tea. He chugged back half the glass without taking a breath and set it down, wiping his lips with the back of his hand.

"It must be good," Patricia said, coming out of her trance.

He handed her a glass. She sipped in her dainty way, one sip, then two, then three. Roland handed her a napkin. She handed him her glass, took the napkin in her right hand, and swiped the back of her left hand across her moist lips. They shared a smile, then her eyes went cold. Her smile disappeared behind tight lips that were no more than a border for the slit that concealed her mouth.

"Do you need anything else?" Roland asked.

"The old one walked away after that. I guess he felt he had made his point. Bernhard ran down the stairs and into the street. I have no idea where he got it, but when he got out there, he had a woodsman's axe, and he knew how to use it.

"I followed him. He had a box of those fire bottles by the door, and I dragged them to the porch. I was never much for sports, but those creatures came nowhere near me once I lit the wick on the first bottle.

"The others began to fight back after Bernhard had killed two with that axe. Some of them gathered up burning debris that had fallen from the burning church. A couple of men had rifles and took target practice at the monsters' heads. They didn't die from the head wound but it turned them stupid, and they were an easy kill after that.

"Counting Auntie, seven vampires found peace that night. Nine more citizens of Kings Shore died in the ruckus. Nine people with families and destroyed futures.

"Bernhard carried that axe to every victim. He made sure none of them walked off in the night to join the old one. The vampires were stacked like cordwood in the middle of the street and set afire. Auntie's remains had been consumed by the blaze at the church. That left six bodies in that demonic pyre.

Chapter 63

Roland arrived at Patricia's before 7:00 a.m. It was the first time she hadn't been waiting to greet him on his arrival. He wasn't surprised to find the door unlocked.

"Patricia," he called upon entering the foyer.

When she didn't reply he ran to the top of the stairs, taking them two at a time. "Patricia?" he repeated. Still no reply.

With tentative steps, Roland made his way down the hall to her room. He tapped on the door and again called her name.

For the second time, he pushed her bedroom door open, terrified what he might find. If he discovered her lifeless form, he didn't think he could bear it.

Roland stuck his head in and called her name for the third time.

"Come in, dear," came a voice that sounded more like a croak than a voice.

"Are you okay?" Roland asked.

"Oh, I think I will be as soon as I get myself up and moving. I think I could use a bit of help getting started, if you don't mind."

As gingerly as he dared, Roland took her arm, and she maneuvered herself to the edge of the bed. Patricia's feet dangled almost a foot from the floor as she sat, gathering her breath from the effort.

"Are you sure you shouldn't take a day to rest?" he asked her.

She didn't answer him, just extended her hand. Roland took it, and she slid off the bed to her feet. With a groan, the old woman stood. Roland walked beside her until she got to her bathroom.

"I can take it from here, dear," she said. "Why don't you go get some tea started? I will be down very soon."

"I'll come and get you," Roland told her.

"Nonsense, if I need any help I will call you. Now go get that tea started."

Patricia was true to her word. After she got up and moving, she was able to get herself ready. Roland found himself agonizing over the snail's pace Patricia had, getting to her bathroom. When I get that slow, just shoot me, he thought.

An hour later, they were sitting at the small table in the kitchen eating scrambled eggs and toast.

"I know I said it already, Roland, but you will make a fine catch for some nice girl," Patricia said as she finished the last of her eggs.

"I don't know about that," he said. "Scrambled eggs and toast are about as complex as my kitchen skills get."

While Roland cleaned up the kitchen, Patricia padded her way to the porch. When he joined her, she was sitting comfortably, looking out over the land.

"Are you ready to hear the rest of my tale?" she asked him when he sat next to her.

"I am not sure I am," he said. "But we have come too far to stop. Wouldn't you say?"

"Indeed I would."

She looked to the table between them. Her journal lay open. The ribbon marking her page swayed in the breeze. Scuba lay stretched out on the porch swing overseeing everything.

"We found them. Bernhard called it a nest. What a dreadful thing. I could not look into the trees at a nest of robins the same way again.

"It was in the basement of the Steen house. We should have thought of it sooner. We all thought the stories were rubbish, but as it turns out, evil lives on that land."

"Is that..."

Before he could finish, Patricia nodded. "The very same. That is why I told you to stay clear of that place. I had to send you there once so you would feel it. But you should not ever go back there.

"We found seven of them in that house. Most were once people I had known from town. They were mothers and fathers, sisters and brothers. The eldest might have been fifty, and the youngest, just a teenager.

"Bernhard barked out instructions, and the men from town dragged each of those people from the house. They didn't put up any fight. A couple of them hissed like feral cats, but in the end, all those bodies were pulled from the house by their ankles.

"When the sun's rays touched exposed skin, the screaming came. The ones in the house hissed louder when the sound of vampires in agony filled the day. A swirling breeze carried that sick scent into the house, and everyone in there began to cough and gag.

"They were all dragged into the sunlight. By the time they got the last one out, the air was thick with that black foulness. The smell was so horrible, I thought I would faint dead away. Bernhard tried to convince me to go back to town, but I refused to leave his side.

"After the last of them had burned up in the sun, Bernhard began to search the house. The other men assured him there were no more, but he would not give up.

"'The old one was not in there,' Bernhard said. 'Until we find him, this will not be over.'"

Scuba jumped down from the swing and trotted around to the back of the house. Patricia began another editorial on the independence of cats, and that morphed into a string of off-topic anecdotes. Roland sat quietly, while Patricia rambled on about all manner of unrelated subject matter. She had displayed many stalling methods in the days he spent with her, and he recognized this as one of those times.

When she finished, Patricia patted Roland on the hand. "Now, Roland, I think we should go inside for a bit."

Chapter 64

"I think it would be best if you moved your things into one of the guest rooms," Patricia said when they went to the kitchen for lunch.

"I don't think that would be right," Roland answered. "I am already getting strange looks from some of the people around here."

"What people?"

"The young doctor for one," Roland said through a chuckle. "They think I am here to take advantage of a senile old woman."

"Anyone who knows me knows I am anything but senile."

"And still they give me mistrusting looks."

Patricia picked the phone up from the cradle and pushed a speed dial number. "Dr. Mark," she said into the phone. "Patricia Owens. I am quite fine, I assure you. Yes, I agree with you, I do need some help out here. Yes, I do have somebody in mind. You have already met him. I am sure you are, but I know who is best. Yes, yes, if I feel the need for a trained medical person, I will depend on you to recommend someone. For now, Mr. Millhouse is the person I need. He will be retrieving his belongings today, and he will stay here until I contact you. Thank you, doctor. Yes, goodbye."

"Do you think that is all it takes?" Roland asked.

"I can't say that you will not get odd glances, but I guarantee you will not run into any problems."

"Don't mess with Patricia Owens," Roland said, holding his glass up in a mock toast.

She winked but said nothing.

"Shall we continue then?" Roland said.

"Let's get comfortable first. The parlor is about right, I think."

It took Roland about ten minutes to get her settled in her best chair, fetch the journal from the porch, and bring a tray adorned with iced tea and glasses from the kitchen.

"Good?" he asked.

Patricia nodded and began.

"Bernhard refused to leave until we found him. The 'old one,' he kept calling him. It was a man, or at least at some point in its past, it was a man.

"Some think it had to be Malachi Adams. Nobody could dispute that, or prove it. It was too fantastic for me to believe back then. I do believe it now."

"Did you find him?"

"We tore that house apart. He wasn't in it. Bernhard refused to give up. By the time we finished with the house, it was almost dusk. He insisted we search the buildings.

"'That won't be necessary,' someone yelled.

"He tossed his torch into the barn. It went up like it was doused in kerosene. Moments later there came a scream like nothing this world has ever produced.

"Every one of us cringed, covering our ears. We pushed in toward each other, like herd animals do when a predator is near.

"They came right out of the flames. By this time it was past end of day. Not completely dark, but the sky had gone purple, and the trees were just shadows against the purple horizon in the west.

"In the near dark, the things were grotesque. White flames through-out, with that black smoke spewing from deep inside the fire. They ran all about us. The heat, even from several yards away burned my skin. A couple of them passed close by before succumbing to the flames, and I thought

I might pass out from the heat.

"When the last of them fell to the ground in lifeless smoldering silence, it showed itself. The old one I mean. No one saw where it came from. It was like magic the way it appeared before us. All the bravado left even the most aggressive men in our group.

"In a flurry of motion that demon grabbed a young man named Sean O'Flannigan from behind. With a thrust of his talon-like hand, he plunged his fingers into Sean's chest and pulled out his heart.

"I knew then that we had stayed too long. We should have retreated to town, and returned in the morning to finish them."

"They would most likely have changed hiding places," Roland said.

"I'm sure that is what Bernhard thought too.

"It picked Sean up like a sack of grain and began to swing him back and forth. He used the poor man's body as a club, beating his way through the crowd.

"Bernhard lit one of his fire bottles, but that thing threw Sean's corpse at him. The bottle was knocked out of Bernhard's hand, crashing to the feet of Philip Lambert. Philip's clothes caught fire, and he screamed. Oh, how he screamed. Somebody tackled him and snuffed the flames by log-rolling him across the ground.

"He recovered from those burns. The scars were hell to look at, but at least he lived.

"While our attention shifted to Philip, the monster seized the Chabot twins. Those boys were just sixteen, but as big as their daddy. The noise it made, when that demon crashed their skulls together. The heads exploded, blood and brains just sprayed out in all directions.

"Jean Chabot ran at the thing, determined to kill it for what it had done to his boys. That was good news for Bernhard. Jean Chabot only had the attention of the old one for a moment, but that was enough. Bernhard ignited another of his fire bottles, and this time it found the mark.

"The air all around us seemed to be sucked into the flames making a hollow 'whoosh.' Jean Chabot had gotten too close, and the white flames all but consumed him. The foulest black smoke rose from the old one.

"It didn't scream like the others. It growled like a rabid dog. It turned in circles, and I was sure it was studying our faces so it could get revenge. Then it leaped into the air and landed in the well.

"We just stood there, in disbelief, watching the black smoke rise up from the mouth of that well. I could feel myself shaking in Bernhard's arms.

"'Is that it?' somebody asked.

"'I think it might be,' Bernhard said. 'I think it just might be.'

"'Amen,' someone hollered."

Chapter 65

Patricia closed her eyes and tipped her head up toward the sky as though looking to heaven for divine help. Roland sat in silence, waiting for her to continue.

When she opened her eyes, he said, "That wasn't it, was it?"

"If only it were," she said, barely above a whisper.

"Black smoke spewed from the mouth of that well as though the earth was vomiting out the vilest of substances. The white flames illuminated the smoke giving it a ghastly look. The worst, though, was the smell. I can't say that it smelled like this or that. I have not smelled anything before or since with the foulness of that smoke."

Patricia covered her face with her left hand and winced. The memory of that night was so dreadful, Roland had no doubt that Patricia could actually smell the stench of that night all over again.

"Bernhard insisted we cover the well. He was sure the thing died, but Bernhard lived on the side of caution," she continued.

"He walked right over to the edge and peered in. A few of the other men shimmied up beside him, craning to look in, but not getting close enough to see anything.

"That big rock, the one covering the well," Patricia said, looking at Roland.

"You know the one I mean."

He nodded without saying a word.

"It's the same rock that covered the well when Malachi Adams was interred in that well.

"'Let's move that rock over the hole,' Bernhard shouted to everyone.

"I think the thing down there heard him," Patricia said. "No sooner had the last syllable escaped his lips, when up from the darkness and smoke it came. Still burning that white-hot flame, and billowing that awful black smoke. A cacophony of screams filled the night as that thing grabbed Bernhard, and pulled him down into the well with him."

Her voice quivered as she spoke. Patricia didn't know Bernhard long, but it was clear that she loved him deeply. Not the way a woman would love her husband. More like a very dear uncle. Roland reached over and held her hand until she was ready to continue.

"It took two big strong men to stop me from running to the well. I yelled at them, 'He needs help!' but nobody would go near the well after that. And who could blame them?"

"They were afraid," Roland said.

Patricia nodded and said, "We were all terrified. The fear of suffering the same fate as Bernhard took over everyone who witnessed that last desperate act of vengeance. There was no more talk. The men used hand signals to communicate. They retrieved a team of horses and fashioned levers from iron bars, and before another hour passed, that well had been sealed with a rock no creature, no matter how supernatural, could lift."

"Jesus," Roland said under his breath.

Patricia opened her journal. Roland was forever amazed at how she seemed to be able to produce the thing out of thin air. He remembered it being on the porch. He remembered it being in the kitchen. Now, here it was, ready for her.

Patricia's Journal—Thursday, August 1, 1912

Kings Shore is like a ghost town. So many lost. Mother and Father. Auntie and Bernhard. At night, as I lay in the dark in this empty house, I can't breathe. I may never sleep again.

"Do you know what, Roland?" she said with cheer in her voice.
"What?"
"I think, tonight I will sleep just fine."

Chapter 66

Patricia Owens slept. She slumbered the peaceful sleep of an infant. Roland slept in the study with her journal in his lap. The bright morning sun woke him after 7:00 a.m. He woke confused and delirious, unsure where he was or why he was there.

After a moment of taking in the room, when his mind woke enough to reason, Roland Millhouse grew anxious. The warm sweat on his skin suddenly chilled as a wave of nervous perspiration soaked his clothes.

He had only risen before Patricia once in all the visits he'd had in this house. He took the stairs three at a time, tripping over the last and sprawling headlong to the floor. The threadbare rug running the length of the hall left carpet-burned skid marks on his hands and knees.

Ignoring the pain, Roland sprang to his feet and sprinted the length of the hall to Patricia's door. The door was closed. His socked feet skidded across the rug. He had to brace his hands on the doorframe to stop from crashing face first into the solid oak panels. The impact on his already injured hands sent another jolt of searing heat into his flesh.

Now standing in front of the door, he stood too terrified to enter. He looked at the knob, and when he thought about reaching for it the pain in his hands finally registered in his brain. He held them in front of his face. From his wrists to his fingertips, the skin on Roland's hands was pink.

Tiny drops of blood no bigger than the head of a pin dotted the base of his wrist.

He stared, transfixed, at the small drops for a moment. The blood looked so dark, almost black. The dim light in the hall gave the blood the appearance of crude oil. That is what he told himself, it was the light, not the evil.

Instead of letting himself in, Roland tapped gently on the door. She did not answer. He rapped a bit harder. Still no reply.

"Patricia?" he whispered through the wood. "Patricia," he called louder still.

After yelling her name several times, Roland let himself into her room. He knew without having to check her pulse, but he tried anyway. Roland placed his middle and index fingers on her neck. He shuddered at the feel of her cold flesh. He moved his fingers up and down, left and right. He tried to find a pulse in her wrist. He put his ear in front of her face, listening for a breath.

He sat next to her on the bed and picked up her cold hand in both of his.

"Good for you," Roland said, looking at her aged face.

He thought that today, Patricia Owens looked every bit of her 120 years. He also thought her face held the look of complete serenity. He imagined that Patricia knew the moment her heart beat for the last time, and she smiled with that knowledge. With the thought that she would be joining her beloved parents and her auntie, she smiled. Maybe she would even meet up with Bernhard and her long-lost fiancé.

A tear breached the lower lid of his left eye, and he wiped it with the back of his hand. The thought of not ever talking to this woman who he just now realized he dearly loved, left him empty.

Chapter 67

Roland sat in the Huron Room of the MacDonald Funeral Home in Kings Shore. He sat alone in one of the seats normally reserved for immediate family. Patricia Owens had no immediate family. As far as anybody in Kings Shore knew, she had no family at all.

It was ever so much more amazing then, that aside from those seats normally reserved for immediate family, the Huron Room had not a single empty chair. At the back and at both sides of the room, men dressed in dark suits lined the walls.

When the Prime Minister entered with his entourage, few people other than the media took notice. Every person there looked to the front. Few had known Patricia, really known her. They all knew of her, however, and what she meant to the town.

The Prime Minister walked to the front of the room and stood before the podium.

"You all knew Miss Owens better than I. I have read so many wonderful things about this grand lady on my way here from Ottawa. She was, until her passing, the world's most senior citizen. She meant a great deal to this area, and to the country. I know she will be missed."

When the Prime Minister and his wife sat next to Roland, he gave them both a nod of recognition, then returned his gaze to the floor. He couldn't stand to look at the closed coffin containing the remains of his dear friend.

Roland took little notice of the pastor when he stepped up to the lectern. He may have been touched by the heartfelt words delivered with the smooth consoling voice of a grieving friend. He might have been if he had stayed in the room. Roland had closed his eyes and went to a place he didn't know existed. A quiet place, where it was okay to be sad, and nobody expected you to be strong. He consoled himself, thinking it was the same place she went all those times when the mood got too dark.

Roland stayed in that place until he heard his name. He expected to be called on, but the suddenness of hearing his own name gave him a start. He looked into the minister's eyes. Pastor Beaton was an old man, with white hair and a stooped posture. His black suit had none of the sleekness of Roland's clothes. He gave Roland a grin, meant to put him at ease.

Roland stood and walked to the front of the room. The pastor greeted him with a hug, then left Roland on his own in front of a congregation he did not know. He looked at the Prime Minister and his wife. He scanned the rest of the room. He saw many familiar faces, none he knew well, but faces he could recall from his time in town.

"Patricia," he began. "Miss Owens asked me to say a few words. Many of you will recognize me as the news guy who has been up at Miss Owens' place. I came here to say happy birthday to an old woman, take a few pictures and go back to Toronto. But once I met Patricia Owens, once she began to tell me her story, I could not leave until I heard the whole thing. And what a story this grand lady could tell."

"Here, here!" someone called out.

Roland placed Patricia's journal on the lectern. He gently opened the book to a page marked by her ribbon. With the same care and affection he'd seen her use many times, Roland smoothed the page. Many in the front rows may have thought his gesture looked more like a caress than simply smoothing the page.

Roland read:

Patricia's Journal—Sunday, September 1, 1912

I have been so alone here without Mother and Daddy. I miss Auntie and even Bernhard. So many have been taken that I could easily give up and let death take me. I shan't do that. Kings Shore needs everyone to work as one to recover from this ordeal. We shall overcome.

Roland paused, looking over his shoulder at the casket. "That was the last thing she wrote in this journal. She has many others, but this journal tells us so much about not only Patricia Owens, but about all of you."

Roland closed the journal, picked it up and walked from the room.

Chapter 68

Roland sat on the front porch of the old house looking out toward the road. His things were packed. His bag was stowed in the trunk of the Bimmer. He had his story; now he could go back to Toronto, grovel at the feet of the network brass and hope they let him come back. He was due the time off, but the way he left was definitely not protocol.

He sipped from his glass. The last batch of lemonade Patricia would ever make. She made the best lemonade, and Roland wasn't leaving until he finished the pitcher. He would not let one of her last acts be wasted.

Scuba snuck up on him while he stared into the distance. The cat leaped up on Roland's lap and curled into a ball. Roland tensed a bit at first, then unconsciously stroked the cat's fur.

"What are you going to do now, Scuba, old boy?"

Almost like the cat knew he was being addressed, Scuba began to purr.

"Exactly right," Roland said. "Exactly right."

Just then a black Lincoln Town Car kicked up a cloud of dust making its way up to the front of the old mansion. When the dust settled, Roland recognized James Renier, Patricia's attorney.

"Mr. Millhouse," James said as he stepped up to the front step.

"I'll be leaving in a few minutes," Roland said, still stroking Scuba's head.

"Is that Patricia's lemonade?" James asked.

Roland tipped his glass toward the sky as if to toast his departed host.

"Mind if I have a glass?" James asked.

Roland surprised himself when he looked to the tray and saw a second glass next to the pitcher. He was so used to setting out a tray for two he must have done so this one last time. He filled the glass and handed it to James.

"I wanted to talk to you after the funeral," James said, "but you scurried out of there so quick, I didn't get the chance."

Roland shrugged but remained silent. Scuba's purring and the trees rustling in the breeze were the only sounds.

"Patricia summoned me out here shortly after you arrived in town," James continued. "She asked me to change her final will. I tried to talk her out of it, but…"

"Nobody could talk her out of anything," Roland finished.

James nodded. "Well anyway, she left a parcel of land to you."

Roland's gaze was drawn from the distant sky to the lawyer's eyes. "Land?"

"It's an abandoned farm just up the road, near the cemetery. It's about fifty acres of unused bush with the ruins of an old farm."

"I know the place," Roland said.

"Are you feeling okay, Mr. Millhouse?"

Roland's eyes had opened unnaturally wide and bulged from his face. His whole body went rigid. Scuba hissed and jumped from Roland's lap to the porch railing.

"Christ," James uttered.

Scuba's departure brought Roland back. "I'm sorry," he said. "Was there anything else?"

"She asked me to give you this," James said, handing him an envelope. "She wished you to read this before making any decision on your future plans."

Roland took the letter. Without regard to the man standing before him, Roland opened the envelope. Without question, the letter was in Patricia's hand. He had seen the pages of her journal enough to recognize the familiar scrawl. His vision blurred as his sense of loss renewed with the reading of her words.

> *Dear Roland,*
>
> *I am so very sorry to place this burden on you. In all the years passed since the loss of my family, I have not cared for anyone the way I have you.*
>
> *I see great strength in you, so I am confident that I have chosen wisely. The farm with the well is now yours. If I had not left it to you, it may have ended up in the hands of unsuspecting souls who would find more than a nice view when they tried to tame the ground there.*
>
> *You need not keep watch over the land there. The evil that draws you to it is like a repellent to all who pass by. I have sat on that bench and watched cars accelerate when they drew near it. I have seen young people cross the street to get farther away.*
>
> *Just leave it go wild and I think the evil will go dormant again.*
>
> *Wishing you a long and happy life,*
>
> *Patricia*

Roland folded the letter, slid it back in the envelope, and returned his attention to James.

James finished the last of his lemonade, then said, "Yes, one last thing. Patricia has granted you a one-year lease of this house and its contents. The lease is for one dollar. She said you would need a place to stay while you wrote her story. Of course, since you are under no obligation to write any story, if you choose not to, the house will immediately be signed over to Kings Shore."

"Isn't she something?" Roland said.

"I'm sorry?"

"From the grave, she's still getting people to do her bidding," Roland said with a grin.

"Again," James insisted, "you are under no obligation."

"Do you know her story, James?" The man shook his head.

"The story must be told."

With that, Roland stood, picked Scuba up from the railing, and went inside.

ABOUT THE AUTHOR

Mick Ridgewell lives with his wife Lynn, son Cory, and daughter Lauren, in Southern Ontario, where he is currently working on his next novel.

Mick is glad to hear from all his readers. He will receive your email at mickridgewell@yahoo.ca. He can also be found on Facebook or you can follow him on Twitter @mickridgewell.

For more vampire goodness to sink your teeth into,
be sure to check out...

"I killed my parents when I was thirteen years old."

And now, with the murder of Missy Blake twenty-two years later, it's time for Jack Greene to finish what he started.

When the co-ed's mutilated body is found, the police are clueless, but Jack knows what killed the pretty college student; he's been hunting it for years. The hunt has been going on for too long, though, and Jack wants to end it, but he can't do it alone. The local police aren't equipped to handle the monster in their midst, so Jack recruits Major Kelly Langston, and together they set out to rid the world of this murdering creature once and for all.

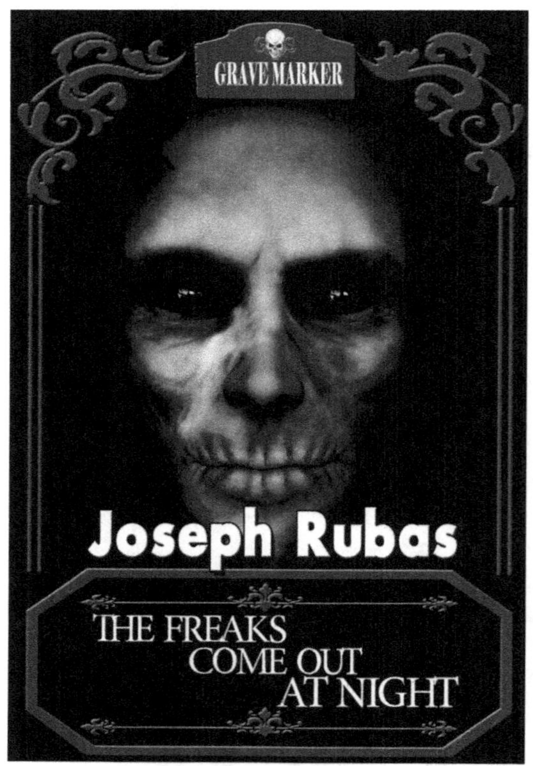

The Mole People have long been part of New York City's mythology. An urban legend, much like the alligators in the sewers. But the Mole People are no myth; they are real, and they are being recruited into an Army of Darkness with one purpose: to claim the city for its own.

Frank Burger, a NYPD homicide detective, and Harvey Goldblum, a paranormal investigator, have both uncovered the plot, but when they reveal the truth, will anybody believe them? Or will the lights of Broadway go forever dark? Will the City that Never Sleeps become a playground for the undead?

www.ingramcontent.com/pod-product-compliance
Lightning Source LLC
Chambersburg PA
CBHW070921190726
48292CB00004B/1051